YOU MADE ME LOVE *You*

D. Brown-Newton

Copyright

Chapter One

Jess

"Why don't you answer the phone and put that girl out of her misery?" I confronted Tristian about his phone that kept ringing.

Tristian is my friend and he has been at my place for two days, ignoring his girlfriend, Toni's, phone calls. She's been blowing up his phone and even calling my phone a few times; cursing me out like it was my fault he wasn't answering her calls. I keep telling him that he's going to mess around and have me snap her neck if he doesn't check her ass. I be trying not to go there with her, because like I said; he's my friend and I try to be respectful of his girl, but she be doing too much when she's mad at him. She's been with him for a year so she should already know that this is what he does when she pisses him off. But, instead of letting him be to calm down, this is what she does.

"Nah, I'm not fucking with her right now because she on that bullshit," he said, flicking through the channels.

"Well, I'm going to need you to take your cock-blocking ass home," I said jokingly.

I haven't been able to hang out or Netflix and chill because he refuses to take his behind home and deal with his annoying girlfriend.

"You know you like chilling with a nigga, because I'm not like none of those lame ass dudes you be fucking with," he laughed.

"Well, those lame ass dudes keep my bills paid, so unless you're cutting a check to management this month; it's time for your ass to get gone," I lied, because I pay my own bills.

"I'm not trying to hear all that; you need to take your ass in that kitchen and fry that chicken, and make sure you dip it in the pancake mix the way I like it," he ordered.

"Tristian, you have a whole fucking girlfriend at home. I'm not your personal chef, so take your ass home like I've been saying, before I invite her over here," I told him, picking up his hoodie that was on my floor, throwing it at him.

"You got my place looking crazy, like you don't know how I hate it when you throw your shit all over the place," I snapped, walking into the kitchen to fry him some chicken.

Tristian knew that I had a soft spot for his ass so if he wanted chicken, chicken was what he was going to get. Just as I was about to dip the last few pieces of chicken into the pancake mix, I heard banging at my front door. When I walked into the living room, Tristian sat his narrow behind there like he didn't hear it.

"I know you hear someone knocking on the door," I said to him.

"Yeah, I hear it but this is your damn crib, so what I look like answering your door?" he chuckled.

"It never stopped you before," I shouted over my shoulder.

"Can you please tell Tristian to come to the door?" Toni said with a roll of her eyes as soon as I opened the door.

"Look, don't be bringing no attitude to my front door," I barked at her ass.

"I said please and trust, if I had an attitude you would know," she snapped.

"Tristian, you better get your girl," I told him, leaving her ass at the door and walking back to the kitchen, trying to keep my attitude that could match hers in a matter of seconds in check.

I had chicken to fry and didn't have time to be getting in the middle of her and Tristian's beef when it didn't concern me. It wasn't like they weren't going to be making up like they always did, so getting in the middle would be a waste of my time. When I came out of the kitchen, Tristian was sitting back in his favorite spot on the couch, so I guess he said something she wanted to hear because I didn't hear any arguing.

"So, I take it she fell for whatever bullshit you just fed her, huh?" I asked with a raised eyebrow.

"Stop fronting like you don't know," he smirked.

"Know what?" I asked him.

"You're acting like you don't know I'm that nigga." He got up going into the kitchen.

"If you say so, Tristian," I smiled, following him into the kitchen.

After we finished eating, he said he was finally going home. I'm not going to say that I wasn't a bit disappointed, because I was. He was right about me fronting when I said that I wanted him to leave, because I enjoyed his company, but I guess it was time for him to get back to his life with his girlfriend. I stayed in the kitchen to clean up, so he shouted from the living room that he was leaving and when I finished

4

up, I went to lock the door. After locking the door, I walked back into the living room to straighten up and I saw that he left money on the table. I picked up the money and it was nine hundred dollars, the exact amount for next month's rent. He knew I didn't mean anything by that statement I made, because I was just fucking with him, so I texted him.

Me- You know that I was just fucking with you; you didn't have to leave me any money.

Tristian- Stop tripping and just say thank you, shorty.

Me- Thank you.

Tristian- Later.

I smiled at the thought of his ass, as I sat the phone back down on the table, because he always came off to others as rough around the edges, but he really wasn't. After I finished cleaning up, I went upstairs to take a shower because I had to be at work in the morning. Now that he blessed me with next month's rent, I think that I might treat myself to a new purse or some shoes, because I deserved it. All I do is take my ass to work and most of the time, I'm too tired to even hang out, but this weekend I'm going to enjoy myself. Instead of going to bed when I got out of the shower, I stayed on the phone with Tristian's crazy ass until I could no longer keep my eyes open.

"Tristian, I'm tired; I'll talk to you tomorrow," I whined.

"You must have a nigga coming over, because you're rushing me off the phone," he insinuated.

"I don't have anyone coming through, but I do have to be to work early tomorrow," I told him.

"Now I know you bullshitting, because that never stopped you before from talking to me before," he said, sounding like he was getting upset.

He didn't even let me respond before saying he'd holla at me later and ended the call with his rude ass. I have no idea what was up with him, but he was beginning to act like I was his girl and not Toni, who is his current girlfriend. I do know that most of his arguments with her were because of our friendship, but she needed to understand that we were only friends.

The next morning, I dragged my feet because I was tired from sitting on the phone with Tristian all night. I started to call in but I was about my paper, so that was an afterthought as I headed to the bathroom to handle my business.

I work at a law firm as a receptionist, making good money. My boss, Luke Bronson, is a high-profile criminal lawyer. His clients were mostly thugs, as I like to call them and it's not a day that goes by that I'm not getting complimented or asked out. When I first started working there it was flattering, but now it's becoming annoying with the unwarranted attention. I haven't met so many thirsty niggas in my life and I swear; it was becoming a turnoff for me. They needed to be worried about concentrating on their cases and staying out of trouble, instead of trying to get hooked up.

My dad had an issue with me working for the infamous Luke Bronson, because he feels that he keeps criminals that should be behind bars on the street. I told him it's a job and he knows I'm about my paper, so unless he's going to pay all my expenses the B & B Law Firm is where I'm going to be working. I love my boss and I love what inspired him and his brother to even start their own law firm. When Luke was sixteen and his brother was fourteen, their father was convicted of a crime that he didn't commit and was sentenced to life in prison. Back then, his father couldn't afford representation, so he was appointed a Legal Aid attorney that did nothing to help his case. Their father was killed two years later in prison, so Luke and his brother, Vernon, went to law school vowing to own their own law firm one day and they succeeded. I tried to explain that to my father and let him know that although most of his clients are in the life, he does represent clients from all walks of life. My boss and his brother's motto has always been innocent until proven guilty, so they don't judge; they just do what they are paid to do.

I arrived at work twenty minutes early so I went into the breakroom to have a cup of tea and a bagel before starting my day.

"Good morning, Jessica," Reagan, who was Luke's assistant, said dryly.

I couldn't stand her ass, just like I knew the feeling was mutual. I've been working here for about a year now and she never liked that Luke took a liking to me. The first day I started this job, she was showing shade before she even got to know me. I think it had to do with my calling my boss, Mr. Bronson, and he told me to call him Luke. Since that day, she just decided that she didn't care for me and decided to do all kinds of petty shit. She's so stupid, because the only reason he told me to call him Luke was although his brother wasn't in the office much, it didn't make sense to be calling them both Mr. Bronson. Luke is old enough to be my father, so trust me; I'm not and have never been interested in nothing other than him being my boss. So, she didn't have to worry about me interfering by messing with her sugar daddy.

Chapter Two
Toni

I was up getting ready for work and Tristian was still sleeping, and just looking at him pissed me off. I went to bed at eight and he thought I was sleeping, but I wasn't, just lying down with my eyes closed like most nights. I knew that he stayed on the phone with Jess all night. I promise you that when I first met Tristian, I was bothered that he had a female friend. As the months went on, I didn't see a reason to be bothered because the friendship seemed genuine, but I must say that these last two months, he's been acting like she was his girl. He was cool whenever she wasn't seeing anyone, but I noticed that he starts getting clingy whenever she does start seeing someone.

This stunt he pulled by staying at her place for the last two days had nothing to do with me tripping, but that's what he tried to get me to believe. Jess told him that she was being treated to Atlantic City by one of her male friends she kicks it with from time to time, so he called himself blocking. He doesn't know that I overheard him on the phone, copping an attitude with her when she told him about it. I knew why he was at her place, that's why I got upset and showed up at her place. But all it did was make me feel as if he didn't care, being that he didn't leave with me. I don't know how much more of him I can take treating me like I'm just something to do when she's unavailable.

He got upset last night when she wanted to get off the phone, like he didn't have a girlfriend in the room that he could have been spending time with. I didn't have time to have a conversation with him this morning because I had to get to work, but I will be discussing it with him when I get home this evening. I work at Chase bank downtown, so I had to get going if I wanted to make it to work on time. I was going to text him later to let him know that I needed him to be home when I got off, because I needed to talk to him.

"Hey girl, did that man of yours bring his ass home?" my co-worker, Demayo, whispered.

"He's home but he could have stayed where he was at, because all he did was leave her house to come home, but stayed on the phone with her all night," I stressed.

"You have to start putting your foot down because he's running all over you, because you're allowing it. Let my nigga think it's cool to stay at any female house for two days, then come home and sit on the phone with her all night. Do you think he's fucking her?" she asked me.

"I don't know," I sighed.

"Well, that's something you need to ask him because this shit is getting crazy, because his actions is saying that something is going on," she suggested.

"Trust, I will be having a conversation with him tonight," I told her before going to clock in.

I tried to get through the day and not focus on Tristian, but I'd kept my feelings bottled up for too long. Nobody knew how many sleepless nights I done had behind his ass because I stay smiling; pretending shit was all good just to avoid looking insecure. I'm to the point to where I don't care how I come off anymore, and if Tristian wants me to continue being his girl, he needs to start treating me that way.

When I got home, I knew that Tristian wasn't going to be home because he never responded to the message I sent him earlier. After changing my clothes, I went downstairs to the kitchen to make some dinner, just to keep my mind off how mad I was and the fact that I was hungry. This situation with Tristian's ass was weighing heavy on my mind, so I didn't even bother eating lunch today and now I was starving. My phone rang and I only answered it because it was my mother calling.

"Hey, Mom," I answered, trying to sound like my bubbly self but failing miserably.

"How you feeling? I haven't heard from you in a couple of days," she said and she wasn't lying, because I wasn't trying to talk to anyone.

"I'm fine, Mom," I lied.

"Well, you don't sound fine and you know that I don't meddle in your business, but what's going on with Tristian and that girl? You know on Mondays, I have an early dinner with a few of the church members after the meeting ends and I saw him with her. I know you say that's his friend, but it just didn't sit right with me because if he's going to take her out to Junior's, I just think that you should be invited too. I wanted to approach him, but with these old legs of mine by the time I would have made it over to the other side, he would have been gone being they were leaving the restaurant," she said and my angry tears fell.

I have been trying to convince my family that Jess and Tristian were just friends; they didn't believe it but they accepted it. Now here I go looking stupid again, because I had no idea that they were even hanging out this evening.

"Mom, I'm going to call you back," I told her, ending the call.

I wiped at my tears before going to call his phone, but he walked through the door with the evidence in his hand.

"Hey, I didn't know you were going to Junior's. No invite?" I questioned, because I literally worked a few blocks from the restaurant.

"Junior's not your spot, so that's why I didn't even ask you," he claimed.

"So, Junior's is Jess' spot?" I questioned, with a raised eyebrow and a twist of my lips.

"What's that supposed to mean?" he said, getting defensive.

"You said that you didn't invite me because it's not my spot, right? So, since you took Jess, I'm asking you if that's her spot," I repeated.

"Toni, don't start tripping like you always do for no reason. You know Jess and I hang out, so don't make the shit out to be more than what it is," he barked, thinking his getting loud was going to shut me up like it normally does.

"You and Jess been doing a lot of hanging out, so when is it your girl's turn to hang out? I don't know when the last time you spent time with me, or us even having sex, but I need to not make it more than it is. You rather sit on the phone with her all night instead of chilling with me, but it was cool to take her to Junior's today, two blocks from my job and not even invite me. Granted, I don't like Junior's, but how about you not going to Junior's, and stopping by my job and taking me somewhere that you know I like to go?" I spat.

"I'm not about to do this with you right now," he said, agitated.

"Why not now, Tristian? Let me guess; you're hanging out with Jess again, right?" I yelled, getting in his face.

"Yo, I'm out," he blurted out.

And there it was; his favorite comeback, but he wasn't leaving without a fight tonight, because I wasn't having it. All he was going to do was leave and run to her house and tell her that I was tripping again, just because he couldn't keep it real and answer the damn question.

"You're not leaving tonight because I'm trying to talk to you about my feelings and this relationship. I advise you to sit down and hear what I have to say," I told him boldly.

"Toni, you on some backwards ass bullshit accusing me and Jess of more than being friends again. We got past that shit when you realized that we were indeed just friends, so who is in your ear with this bullshit?" he said, but sat his ass back down on the couch.

"Nobody is in my ear, it's your actions and then my mother sees you at Junior's with her today; it's just becoming to be too much. I don't want to fuss or fight with you, but I need for you to understand how this relationship with you and Jess is looking, when you spend more time with her then you spend with me. I want to be treated like your girl and do things that couples are supposed to do together," I said, really getting in my feelings as my tears fell.

"So, you didn't see this shit that I have in my hand when I walked in the door?" he said, holding up a movie he got from the Redbox, causing me to smile.

I knew that I shouldn't have allowed him to worm his way out of the discussion at hand, but being that spending time with me was part of the argument, I decided to let it go for now.

"I just don't understand why you always tripping," he said, pulling me down onto the couch into his arms.

I swear this is all I wanted from him and it felt good to be in his arms, because it's been a while since he held me like this. Being I didn't get to finish dinner, we ordered Chinese food and sat on the couch watching *Fences,* enjoying each other and I loved it. His phone kept vibrating in his pocket and I just knew that he was going to answer the phone, but to my surprise, he didn't. After the movie was over, I picked up the containers so that I could dump them and clean up before heading upstairs.

"Meet me upstairs once you done so that we can take a shower together and really get this night popping," he said, smirking before heading upstairs and causing me to blush with excitement.

When I was done, I walked up the stairs and Tristian was standing in the guest room talking on the phone.

"It's not like that. I'm just spending some time with her because she was tripping on my taking you to Junior's today," I heard him say, then pause. "Don't worry about it. I'll pretend like I'm seeing it for the first time. I have to go, I will holla at you later," he said, ending the call.

I crept back downstairs because I didn't want him to know that I heard his conversation, out of fear of hurting his ass. *So, just to appease me, he made me think that the movie was for us to enjoy, but he got the movie for her.* My tears fell and I was so tired of crying, but to hear that shit, it hurt me to my core. I just didn't understand why he felt the need to lie to me and if he wants everything to be about their relationship, all he had to do was be honest and let me go. I love him to death, but I will not continue to sit back and allow him to treat me like I'm just his fucking roommate. I heard him coming down the stairs so I tried to wipe at my tears quickly, because I didn't want him to see me crying yet again.

"Why the fuck are you sitting here crying when we supposed to be getting it popping?" he barked.

"Tristian, why do you keep doing this to me?" I cried.

"What now, damn," he said, getting frustrated.

"I heard you on the phone talking to Jess and I just don't understand what is going on. Why would you lie to me and tell me that you got that movie for us to enjoy, when it was for the two of you. So, you were only spending time with me because I was tripping? I love you, Tristian, but if this is what our relationship has become, then I think it's best that we end it

17

His entire stance screamed "thug" but I didn't care, because like I said this nigga was fine and he had a bitch in a trance staring at him. Reagan was all up in his face like she wasn't old enough to be his mother. I mean she looked good for her age; she was in her late forties, but that never stopped her ass from flirting with all the male clients being her naturally thirsty self. I walked towards the breakroom like I did every morning and I could feel his eyes following me, so I added an extra switch to my hips until he could no longer see me. I didn't even want a cup of tea or a bagel this morning, because I wanted to get back out front to continue staring at the eye candy that was on display this morning. When I got back to the receptionist area, he was the one doing the staring this time. I tried to avoid eye contact because I started to feel uncomfortable with how his stare alone, was doing something to my body. I tried to focus on the clients that needed to sign in and tell me what lawyer they were here to see, but found myself sneaking glances of him on the low.

I had just finished up on a phone call and when I looked up; he was standing there, causing me to jump a little because he startled me.

"You do know that it's rude to stare and not speak, don't you?" he said with a smile on his face, showing his perfect set of teeth.

Now that he was standing in front of me, I could see that he had a scar on the right side of his face. It wasn't a gruesome scar and it didn't take away from him still being fine to me.

"Well, I would have to ask you the same question, being that I caught you staring as well," I said to him with a smile on my face too.

I couldn't believe that I was flirting with this man at my place of work and it was obvious, because Reagan rolled her eyes with a disgusted look on her face, like she didn't do this shit on a regular.

"What's your name?" he asked me.

"Jess and yours?" I wanted to know.

"Kylief and now that we got that out of the way, shoot me your digits so that we could continue this conversation later. I have some business later, but I'll definitely be hitting you up as soon as it's handled."

I had to think if I wanted to give him my number, being he's clearly at the office having legal woes with the criminal court, but shit, *who was I to judge*? I thought as I slid him my digits. I watched him walk out the door after telling me that he would call me later tonight. I couldn't stop smiling, until Reagan's ass came getting in my personal space.

"Did I just see you give a client your number when you know that it's against company policy?' she asked, causing me to look at her like she was crazy.

She couldn't be serious right now when her ass was fucking Luke, his brother, and a few of the clients. So, for her to come at me on that bullshit, she must have been upset that Kylief was interested in me and not her ass. But why would he be interested in her old ass when my fine ass is sitting here? Bitch, bye.

"I don't know what you think you saw, but all I gave that man was a business card, so I guess that would be a no; you didn't see me give him my number," I told her with a roll of my eyes.

"Just make sure that was all you were giving him, because I would hate to have to report you," she threatened.

One thing that people got misconstrued when it came to me was that I wasn't to be fucked with, but they always learned the hard way. I was a nice person and didn't fuck with no one unless they fuck with me and I swear, she just took me from 0 to 100 threatening me.

"Says the bitch that's fucking everything moving, trying to peg me to be like your trifling ass but trust me; I'm not that thirsty. So, I'm going to need you to get gone before I mop this floor with your old ass," I barked at her.

"I would love to see you try Jess, don't think that because your younger that I'm intimidated by you and trust you won't be mopping the floor with this ass." she stated boldly and just as I was about to step from behind my area we were both being called into Luke office.

I swear, if I lose my job behind her, I promise you that this bitch was going to feel these hands for sure.

"Have the two of you lost your damn mind to be doing this at my place of business like neither of you have any home training? I never expected my two best employees to be conducting themselves in such a manner in front of potential clients. I have a reputation to uphold and I will not have anyone and I do mean *anyone* that works for me destroy what my brother and I work so hard to keep. Now, what was the argument about?" he asked, clearly pissed because I have never heard him raise his voice before.

"I was sitting out at my desk working and she accused me of giving a client my personal phone number. I explained to her that I did no such thing when in fact, I handed him one of our business cards. She said that she didn't care if it was a business card or not, because she was going to report that I was frolicking with a client and that you would believe her. She went on to say that the two of you were dating and that you would believe anything that she told you and that's how the argument started," I said, giving him half the truth.

You see, no one's supposed to know that they are dating but this bitch couldn't hold water, so for me to add that fact, he had no choice but to believe the rest.

"Ms. Jenkins, I need for you to go back to the front," he said to me and I smirked because I knew he was about to get in her ass.

When she finally emerged from his office, she looked like she's been crying and that's what she gets for trying to be all up in my business. After work, I was still kind of pissed off but being I didn't really get reprimanded, I decided to let the shit go. When I exited the building, I was not expecting Kylief to be out front, leaning against his truck. He was no longer dressed like he just left court; he was now wearing a black hoodie, jeans and a pair of the new Retros. His fitted was pulled down but when I got closer, he turned it to the back showing off those sexy eyes of his, causing me to blush.

"What are you doing out here, business hours are over," I said to him.

"Just trying to see what your sexy ass about to get into," he flirted.

"I was just about to go home and get out of these clothes," I said, causing him to lick his lips, but I didn't mean it the way it came off to his ass.

"I didn't mean it like that, so get those thoughts out of your head," I said, shaking my head.

"I was just fucking with you, shorty, but check this out; I just wanted to come holla at you and ask you if I could take you out tonight."

"Don't you think we should get to know each other first being we just met?" I asked him.

"What better way to get to know each other by going out, because I damn sure can't get to know you over the phone. The eyes and facial expressions tell me everything I need to know about a person, so I'll hit you later so we can discuss the politics," he said, looking at me briefly before leaving me standing there as he got in his truck and drove off.

This nigga rude as hell, but I'm not going to lie and say that I wasn't turned on right now, as I walked to my car to take my ass home.

Chapter Four
Jess

When I got home, I was pissed to see Tristian sitting on my couch playing PS4, like I didn't tell him to take that game home where he lives on so many occasions.

"Why are you here, Tristian? I told you that I'm mad at you so you need to leave, and I'm going out so you need to go," I told him.

"Going out where?" he asked, but not telling me why he was here to begin with.

"That's not important and how many times do I have to tell you to only use my key if it's an emergency? What if I had company or was coming home with company? Not a good look, because it's going to look like something that it's not," I fussed.

"It doesn't matter who the fuck you have up in this motherfucker or walk up in here with, because once I stepped through the door, the nigga is going to get escorted the fuck up out of here," he barked.

"The last time I checked, my name is Jess and not Toni, so miss me with all that shit you talking and bounce. I'm serious, Tristian; I'm going out tonight and I need to get ready," I said, needing for him to leave and take his ass home to his girl.

"I asked you a question," he repeated.

"I'm going out with a friend," I said, putting my phone on the charger.

"Which friend, because I know all of your friends?"

"Well, you don't know this one, so stop with all the questions and go. I promise to holla at you later," I said, rushing him.

"Not until you tell me who you're going out with," he insisted and I knew if I didn't tell him something, we would be doing this back and forth all night.

He turned the game off and was now looking at me to answer his question, and I was getting pissed because I hated when he did this. Our friendship was starting to feel like a relationship that I didn't want to be in, because he was starting to act like I was his possession and not his friend anymore.

"Tristian, I'm going out with a dude I met at work today, so I need you to go so that I could get ready," I sighed.

"So, you're going out with some dude that you just met and don't know shit about?" he exploded, but I wasn't fazed by his attitude.

"That's the point of going out with him so that I could get to know him." I explained but I don't even know why I tried because he wasn't going to care.

"I don't think you should be going out with someone you just met, because that nigga could be a killer for all you know. Didn't you just say that you met him at your job? So that says he has a criminal charge."

"Tristian, I understand your concern, but I'm a big girl and I'm going to be ok, so like I said…I have to get ready."

"You're right; I'm sorry for caring, so you be sure to enjoy your night," he said, getting upset leaving out and slamming my door.

I didn't have time to do this with Tristian's ass, because he was acting like a scorned boyfriend right now. He needed to be taking that attitude up with his girl. I went upstairs to shower so that I could at least have that out of the way by the time Kylief called. I didn't pick out anything to wear just yet, because I didn't know where he was going to end up taking me, so after my shower I just chilled until his call came through. Just as I was about to go into the kitchen to get something to drink, my phone rang and I thought it was Kylief, but it was my girl, Trish.

"What's up, girl?" I answered.

"Don't be sounding like we good when I haven't heard from your ass in days, like you don't love me anymore. Anyway, I wasn't calling about that. I was calling because I wanted to know what the hell did you do to my brother? I asked him if he spoke to you and he said, 'fuck Jess', so what's that about?" she asked.

"Your brother thinks that I'm supposed to be at his beck and call and it doesn't work like that. I keep trying to explain to him that I'm not his girl so he can't pimp who I choose to chill with, so he got mad and left," I told her.

"You and Tristian need to get it together with this love-hate relationship the two of you have," she said.

"I don't know about us having a love-hate relationship; he's just been acting so clingy lately and it's annoying. I don't know if it's because of him and Toni not getting along, but the shit is starting to piss me off," I admitted.

"Why is she sitting on the phone talking to you when she said she was going on a date? Tell her ass to go and enjoy herself," I heard Tristian say in the background.

"Tell Tristian to take his ass to work sometimes, he wouldn't have so much time on his hands to worry about what I'm doing," I yelled into the phone.

"I'm the boss, so I don't have to be at work to make money," he yelled back.

"Let me take you off speaker because both of you are doing entirely too much," Trish said, but she shouldn't have had me on speaker anyway.

"Trish, I'm going to call you once I make it home, girl, because I don't have time to breastfeed your brother." We laughed.

"Hold up, missy, you still didn't tell me who you're going out with tonight. You know how we do, so spill the tea," she said, not letting me hang up.

"His name is Kylief. I met him at my job today; he asked me out and I accepted. Oh, and did I mention that he's fine?" I laughed.

"Well, have fun and text me when you make it home. Be safe," she said.

"I will and tell your big head brother I said to take his ass home to Toni and I'll call him tomorrow," I told her before ending the call.

It was going on eight and Kylief still hasn't called me yet and I didn't have his number to call to see if we were still going out. I told myself that I was going to give him thirty more minutes, before I went into the kitchen to get something to eat and call it a night. I swear, he had fifteen minutes before his time was up, when he finally decided to ring my phone. He said that he was running late, so asked me for my address and said that he would be here at nine. So after I got off the phone, I went to get dressed. He didn't mention where we were going, so I just put on a pair of dark blue ripped jeans, with a white tank under my pink twist-front top and finished my ensemble off with my pink, custom-made, Chuck Taylor All Star sneakers. I was looking cute, so all I had left to do was add some accessories and I was ready to go. I needed to hurry because he finally called and said that he was out front. I don't know why I was now standing in the middle of my bedroom, contemplating if I should go out with him or not. I know it was a little too late to be having second thoughts, being that he was here, but that's exactly what I was doing. I think I was letting Tristian get in my head and that wasn't a good thing, so I let all thoughts of him go.

I grabbed my jacket, phone, and bag and left the house, trying to erase all thoughts of Tristian's ass in the process. He wasn't driving the truck he was in earlier and I guess he saw me looking around, so he blew the horn to let me know that it was him in the black Lexus.

"Hey beautiful, how are you?" he asked once I was in the car, causing me to blush.

"Thank you," I responded shyly.

I was so nervous and I think it had to do with me feeling him, because he looked good and he smelled good. His eyes were kind of intimidating too, so I decided that I would avoid eye contact with him, but he wasn't trying to give me that.

"I didn't take you as the shy type," he said, briefly taking his eyes off the road to look at me.

"That's because I'm not shy once we get to know each other better," I said and he smirked before focusing back on the road.

We pulled up to K Lanes near Times Square and they never lied about this being the city that never sleeps. You would have thought it was Friday or Saturday, looking at how packed this place was, like no one had to work in the morning, including myself. I always heard about this bowling alley, but I've never been and I couldn't believe how many bowling lanes they had. They had just as many billiard tables and the live music was giving me life right now. I've been bowling before in Queens where I live, but that place was a hole in the wall compared to this place. Kylief grabbed my hand as we walked to a secluded area that had private lanes, a bar and a DJ station. I couldn't believe that he booked a secluded area just for the two of us and I must say that I was impressed.

Chapter Five
Kylief

"So, all of this for a female you just met?" Jess asked me.

"It's not about me just meeting you; it's about me asking you out, so it's my job to go all out and show you an enjoyable time. So, before I beat that ass in bowling, tell me about you so we could get that out of the way."

"First, let me say that I don't know about you beating my ass in bowling. Now that we got that out of the way, you already know I work at the law firm. I've been there for a while and for the most part, I like working there. I'm twenty-four, an only child besides my best friends, who happens to be sister and brother. My mother passed away when I was three years old, so when my dad worked, their mother babysat me and that's how we all became friends. I'm not dating right now, but I do go out from time to time but nothing serious. So, what about you?" she finished.

"Not much to tell but I'm an open book, so if you ever feel you need to know anything about me, all that I ask is that you ask me. Nobody can tell you better than I could tell you, so what do you want to know?" I said, because I never offer up anything that a person didn't ask to know.

"Are you single? Any kids? Job? Family? I think that covers everything," she smiled.

"I'm single by choice, no shorties, I'm a business owner of this fine establishment that your about to take that L in. I have two siblings on my pop's side, but it's just me and my mom."

"Oh, wow, so this you? I have to say that I'm impressed but it kind of saddens me that you will be taking that L in your establishment. It's a good thing that we are in a secluded area, so your employees don't get to see the boss get his ass beat," she laughed.

"Well, let's get to it and I apologize in advance for spanking that ass, and I hope that you don't hold it against me when I ask you out again."

"Let's do it," she said as she stood, ready to play.

We ended up playing three games and she kicked my ass; shorty wasn't lying when she said she was a beast at bowling. I didn't get to play much, so I was just fucking with her when I told her I was going to beat her. After dinner and drinks, I stepped away for a second to go upstairs to talk to my right-

36

hand man, who handled business when I wasn't in attendance. I needed to let him know that I was about to be out, and good looking on getting the area ready for my date with Jess.

"So, did you have enjoyed yourself?" I asked her once we were back in the car.

"Yes, I really did and the best part was whooping that ass," she boasted.

"Anyway, I had fun with you tonight and I hope that we could do it again. I will say that I'm a busy man but I'm feeling you, so I promise to make as much time as possible for you," I told her, being honest.

"I appreciate that but haven't you heard all work and no play, makes for a boring life and no wife," she joked, displaying that pretty ass smile of hers.

"Baby girl, trust that my life is anything but boring; I just got my mind on the bigger picture right now," I informed her.

"And what might that be?" she inquired.

"I'm chasing that million-dollar dream and I'm not going to stop until I have it, so when I do find that woman I want to wife, trust; she'll be thankful."

"I feel you and I respect the chase," she said, leaning her head back against the headrest as I pulled out into traffic to take her home.

That's the reason I'm single, because I haven't met a female yet that understands the hustle, but time will tell. I was expecting shorty to ask me about my business at her law firm, but she didn't and I respect that shit. When I pulled up to her crib she had already dozed off, so I tapped her lightly to wake her up. I see she's a lightweight when it comes to drinking as she sat there wearing a silly look on her face because she fell asleep.

"You good, lightweight?" I teased.

"I'm good, just tired because you kept me out past my bedtime," she answered.

"Is that right? Are you sure that it doesn't have anything to do with those three drinks you threw back at my spot?" I laughed.

"No, it doesn't have anything to do with those watered-down drinks you're pushing off as straight liquor," she joked.

"My drinks straight fire and I'm seeing the proof live and in color, but I'm going to let you go, and try not to fall asleep at work tomorrow," I told her.

38

"I'm good and thanks," she said, attempting to get out of the car, but I pulled her back and kissed her goodnight before letting her out of the car.

I waited until she was inside before pulling out and taking my ass home, because shorty had me feeling something that I haven't felt in a long time. I needed to keep my head in the game, without distractions, but tonight was a much-needed distraction that I enjoyed. I grabbed my phone from the cup holder and dialed her number.

"Hello," she answered and I cursed myself because I heard the shower water running, letting me know she was about to get in.

"Hey, I just wanted to make sure you made it in ok," I blurted out, which was stupid because she knew that I sat in my car until she made it in.

"It's ok, it's normal to miss me so soon after being in my presence," she laughed.

"Goodnight, Jess," I laughed, ending the call.

I was in the crib no longer then ten fucking minutes, before Demayo was hitting my phone like she didn't understand I'm done. She was one of those chicks that I was talking about when I said they didn't understand the hustle. I never understood how a female wanted a nigga to always be up under them instead of working, so I told her she needed to go and find that buster that she was looking for, because I wasn't him. As soon as I cut her off; she decides she want to get some act right, but I don't back-track so I meant it when I said I'm done. I let her call go to voicemail because all I wanted to do was shower and take my ass to bed, because I had a busy morning tomorrow.

The next morning, I arrived at my mother's house to take her to her doctor appointment that I had to literally fuss with her to make. When I walked in, she was sitting in her recliner drinking her morning coffee, watching the news like she didn't have anywhere to be this morning.

"Good morning, son," she acknowledged, but kept her eyes on the television.

"Mom, why are you still in your robe when you're expected to be at the doctor's office in less than thirty minutes?" I asked her.

My mom was my everything, but sometimes she could be bullheaded and once I get frustrated, that's when she shuts down. That was her thing to avoid doing things that she knew she needed to do, so I made sure not to get frustrated with her, because I really needed her to go to this doctor's appointment. She has been complaining about feeling nauseous every morning and not having an appetite and I was concerned. She has lost so much weight in the last few weeks; we needed to make this appointment, so I had no choice but to be patient with her, so she'd get dressed so that we could go.

"Calm down, boy, I'll be ready in a few minutes," she said, getting up and removing the robe, showing that she was already dressed, causing me to smile.

"I know you thought that you were going to have a tough time with me this morning, didn't you?" she smiled, knowing me well.

"That's because you always give me a tough time when it comes to taking you to the doctor or getting you to get out of the house for a little while," I reminded her.

"You know that I don't like leaving the house and spending money, when I have everything I need right here," she fussed.

"But it's my money, Mom, and I don't mind treating my favorite person sometimes."

"Well, how about you save your money and visit with me more?" she challenged, knowing her visits consist of me watching her watch her stories.

"I promise to spend more time with you, Mom, now let's get going before we get there late," I told her.

Chapter Six
Jess

It's been about two days since my date with Kylief and I haven't spoken to him, but I didn't sweat it because he let me know beforehand that he was a busy man. I walked into work and a beautiful arrangement was sitting on my desk that made me smile. It wasn't a flower arrangement and the smile came about, because he remembered what I told him when we talked about our likes and our dislikes. When he asked me if I liked flowers I told him no, because I thought that buying flowers were a waste of money being that they eventually die. I joked about having a Chico-O-Stick and Peanut Chew arrangement, with a surprise in the middle and well enough, it was sitting on my desk. It was probably corny to everyone else, but Mr. Kylief just earned him some brownie points from me and I couldn't wait to see what the surprise in the middle was going to be. I had no idea that Economy Candy on Rivington Street in Manhattan made arrangements but then again, his ass probably made it happen. I dug my hand into the middle of the arrangement and had to cover my mouth to prevent me from laughing out loud.

Kylief's ass is a character and I swear, he was growing on me and I haven't even known his ass for a week yet. He listens and that's not something that most men are capable of, so he wanted me to know that he didn't just hear me talking, he listened. He served us some jerk chicken wings at the bowling alley and I fell in love with them because they were that good. So, as I was eating the wings, I blurted out that I would sell my ass for some more of those wings, causing us both to laugh. He had a tin of the wings in the middle of the arrangement, with a homemade card with a drawing of a big ass and the words, "That ass belongs to me." Yeah, I know it's corny but I like his corny ass, and he just made my morning. I couldn't wait to get back to my area to give him a call to thank him.

I made it back to my area, even though I wanted to detour to the bathroom and send him a picture of all this ass that he just bought. That would have showed him that I had a sense of humor too, but instead I got my ass to work, but tried calling him to thank him but he didn't answer. I was kind of disappointed that I didn't get to speak to him yet, so I was in a bit of a funk when I left work. When I got home, I saw that

Trish's car was parked out front, which meant she was already inside waiting on me.

"I see you and your brother both don't understand the meaning of using your key for emergency purposes," I laughed.

"Girl, please; you should have known when you gave me a key that I would come as I please," she said.

"I see I'm going to have to revoke your key and let you start sitting in your car and wait until I get home from now on," I told her.

"Anyway, what's that?" she said, ignoring my threatening to take her key as she got up to look at my arrangement.

"This was delivered to my job this morning from Kylief, the guy I told you I went out with the other night," I smiled.

"I like him already, especially if he's going to be supplying us with our favorite candy," she said, taking a few Peanut Chews.

She didn't get to see my surprise in the middle, because I ate my wings for lunch today and I put his note in my bag.

"So, how was the date?" she asked.

"Girl, you know K Bowling Alley that we always said that we wanted to go to?"

"Yeah."

"He owns it and he took me there and had a secluded area where we played the lanes, had drinks and dinner. I had a really fun time with him and I want to see where this could go, if he ever contacts me for our second date," I stated somberly.

"Well, he's interested if his ass sending arrangements to your job. Why don't you give him a call instead of waiting on him to call you?" she suggested.

I wanted to call him but he'd already told me that he was a busy man. I didn't want to be calling him because if he wasn't busy, I'm sure I would have gotten a call by now.

"What's up with your big head brother?" I asked changing the subject, but I was going to ask her anyway because I was low-key missing him.

Tristian and I are both bullheaded, so neither one of us was going to call the other one first, even though he should call being that he was in the wrong. We only had one disagreement before that stopped us from speaking to each other, and that was in high school. He started going out with this female that he knew I couldn't stand because she was always coming for me. I mean, this girl used to fuck with me all the time for no valid reason and he knew how I felt about her. Because he started dating the mean girl, I told him we couldn't be friends. His ass didn't last a day without being friends with me, so he broke up with her that next day. Now, this is the longest we ever went without speaking. Our friendship was more important than anything, so I'm surprised that it was Trish sitting on my couch and not his ass.

"Toni finally reached her breaking point with him about y'all friendship, she feels that he puts you before her and she's not dealing with it anymore. He said that she was upset that he took you to Junior's, because her mother saw the two of you, so I guess her mom made it to be more then what it was," she informed me.

"Toni's been with Tristian too long to be allowing anyone to put those negative thoughts in her head, when she knows were just friends. We're friends and we're going to always be friends, and I don't care who has a problem with it," I said, getting pissed; she knows nothing is going on between us because if it was, I wouldn't have allowed his ass to talk to her at my front door the other day.

"She knows it's nothing, but it doesn't stop her from feeling threatened by the relationship between the two of you.

Tristian spends more time with you than he spends with her and he should understand that when he's in a relationship, he has to know how to separate the two. Also, if he invites you out to a movie or to eat, he should extend the invitation to her as well," she said.

"Trish, she's been with him for how long? She needs to get over this insecure shit when it comes to me and Tristian, because we are just friends!" I screamed out in frustration because it sounded like she was defending Toni.

"So, you really going to act like you don't know that my brother is in love with you and has been since grade school? Just because you put him in the friend zone doesn't mean those feelings just disappeared. You can walk around in denial all you want, but you know what it is, so yes; I understand how Toni is feeling."

"It doesn't matter; we were basically raised like brothers and sisters and yes, I noticed that he has a crush on me, but I will never take it there with him. I love him as my friend and nothing will ever change that, so if Toni is feeling some way then she did the right thing to keep it moving," I spat.

"Yeah ok," she said, twisting her lips and letting me know that she didn't believe me.

"Call him and tell him to come over," I said to her.

"Nope, I'm not getting in the middle of you and Tristian's love spat," she joked.

"Just call him and tell him that I want to see him."

"If you want to see him, call and tell him yourself, like it's going to mean something coming from me. He's going to think I'm lying anyway, because when did you ever need someone to speak on your behalf?" she pointed out.

"You have a point, I guess. I'll hit him up later, but anyway, what we about to get into?" I asked her, ready to Netflix and chill.

"I have to go; I already made plans with Mekhi," she said, causing me to pout.

"I thought that you were staying for a Netflix and chill night, being that we haven't hung out in a while," I whined.

"Nah, I just stopped by to get the scoop on your date," she admitted with her nosey ass.

"Anyway, how are things going with him? Does he still have baby mama drama?" I wanted to know.

She's been with Mekhi for about eight months but out of six of those months, she's been dealing with his baby mama doing petty shit.

"We good for the most part, but his ugly ass baby mama been tripping, like always. She already knows that we're a couple, so my being in the car with him to pick up his daughter shouldn't be a problem, but she made it one. He didn't get his daughter for his weekend visit last weekend, because she was upset that I was in the car. It just makes me think that I should have stuck with my rule of not dating men with children," she stressed.

"Then you would have missed out on a good man and trust that's why she's tripping, because she knows she messed up and now she wants him back."

"I know and that's the reason I'm trying to be patient, but I be wanting to beat that caked-up make-up off her face." We laughed.

"Girl, let me get out of here and don't forget to call Tristian, so that you two could go back to pretending," she joked, running out the door, dodging the pillow I threw at her from the couch.

I tried calling Kylief again to thank him for his thoughtful arrangement, before calling Tristian to see if we could mend our little spat that we had. I didn't tell Trish that I had already tried calling Kylief and he didn't answer, because I didn't want her to tell me what I was starting to think and that was that he wasn't really interested.

"Hey sexy," he answered with his deep voice, surprising me that he picked up.

"Hey, I was just calling to say thank you for the arrangement you had delivered to my job," I said nervously, but had no idea why.

"I thought you said that you weren't dating anyone," he said, leaving me confused at the disappointment in his voice.

"I'm not dating anyone," I said, wondering what he heard.

"Well, who would be sending you an arrangement because I didn't?" he said seriously.

"I-I just thought that it was you because of the candy and the wings that came from your spot," I said on the verge of tears, because I didn't want him to think that I lied to him.

He wasn't saying anything and I didn't know how to make him believe I wasn't dating anyone. I just knew that it was him based on the conversation we had, but now I wasn't sure. I mean, there was a card with the card and the words but there was no name attached. I started to think that it was someone that heard our conversation and was playing a trick, but who? I thought as I started to get pissed. I thought about just hanging up the phone and saying fuck it, because I had no way to prove that I wasn't seeing anyone, but then he spoke.

"Yo, why you so quiet, Jess? I'm just fucking with you." he said, causing me to breathe again.

"That wasn't funny and I'm hanging up now," I said, pretending to be pissed but I was relieved.

"Nah chill, I apologize, but you have to admit that shit was funny and I wish I could have seen the look on your face," he laughed.

"Whatever...you had me second-guessing who the hell could have sent that arrangement to me, even though it had you written all over it," I admitted.

"You should have known it was me, unless you told some other nigga that you loved those candies and my jerk chicken wings. But anyway, that was all me because I was trying to put a smile on your face, being that I haven't seen you in a few days. Let's do something this weekend, if you're not still mad at me."

"I'm not mad, just relieved," I said, being honest.

"Ok, so it's a date. I have to go, but I promise to speak to you before the week is out," he promised, before ending the call.

His ass had a sense of humor on him that made me want to kill him for pulling that stunt, but I like that he had one. I was feeling all warm and bubbly inside at the thought of him and couldn't wait to see him this weekend. I went upstairs to my bedroom to change out of my work clothes before giving Tristian a call, hoping that he didn't ruin the good mood that I was in. I was just going to tell him that we need to set boundaries when it comes to our friendship. I didn't want to cause any more issues for him and Toni, and if I'm going to be dating Kylief, I wanted the same in return.

Chapter Seven
Toni

I was so mad the day I told Tristian I was done, that I've been staying with my mother, just to put some distance between us. She was a pain in my ass with the "I told you so" and that "a male and female could never be just friends" that I took my ass home to get away from her, annoying the hell out of me. When I got home, I was surprised to see that Tristian was home, because I expected him to use this time to spend more time with Jess, like he's been doing. He said that he wanted to talk to me but I was kind of hesitant, because I've heard it all before and he always lived by his words for a few days, before his actions replayed themselves again. But I have to admit; it's been a few days and he's been coming home every day after leaving the shop. I agreed to give us another chance and we were even going out tonight. I couldn't even tell you when the last time Tristian and I have been out on a date, so I was kind of hyped about going out with him tonight.

He agreed to spend more time with me and be mindful of my feelings of his relationship with Jess, and I agreed to stop listening to what others are saying about our relationship and running with it. Demayo did go kind of hard when I told her that I told him it was over, telling me that she felt that I should have been left him but I didn't agree with her. I know that I come off as being jealous of Jess, but I'm just jealous of the relationship that she has with him, because that's the kind of relationship I longed to have with him. She has never been one of those friends that threw their friendship in my face, and she always stayed out of it whenever we got into it about her.

I smiled up at him as I watched him walk into the bedroom; he looked back at me and smiled, just as his phone rang and I knew it was Jess because of the ringtone. I finished applying my make-up as I was doing before he walked into the room. I started to make a fuss about him walking out of the room to talk to her, but I didn't. When I was done getting ready, I grabbed my cell and my clutch, turning out the light before leaving out of the bedroom. He was still on the phone and I heard him saying that he apologizes too and that he never wanted to go this long without speaking again. Well, that explains why he was home the day I came back, and his reason for coming home straight from the shop every day after work.

"Are you ready?" I asked, letting it be known it was time to end his call.

"So, where are we going?" he asked after ending his call.

He couldn't be fucking serious; I bet he never asks Jess where they were going, I thought, but had to remind myself that I was trying to make my relationship work. I knew if I said something of that nature to him, he would have gotten defensive; we would have been arguing and any plans of going out would have been over.

"Where do you suggest we go? I wouldn't mind going out to get something to eat," I offered.

"How about we go to Chops & Sticks," he said, causing a wide ass smile on my face.

"We haven't been there since our first date."

"You remember," he smiled.

"How could I forget the place I fell for the charming man that I later fell in love with?" I gloated at the memory.

"Awww, you about to make a nigga blush," he joked, kissing me on my lips as we headed out the door.

When we arrived at the restaurant, it had changed just a bit; it was no longer buffet-style, it was now dine-in with a wait staff.

"I bet you don't remember what I filled my plate with that night when you joked about me getting your money's worth," I challenged him.

"You had sesame chicken, steamed broccoli, fried rice, wontons, beef lo mein and fried chicken wings. Then you had the nerves to wrap your chicken wings and put them in your bag, because they didn't offer take home cartons," he laughed.

"I was hungry that night and for sixteen dollars for a damn buffet, I wasn't trying to leave those wings behind." I laughed so hard, tears were coming out of my eyes.

"You were walking up out of there like you just robbed a bank, looking around all nervous, like they cared about you taking home some dry ass chicken wings." We both laughed.

"Oh, how I wish we could go back to those days, the days you enjoyed taking me out and being in my presence," I said, hoping he didn't take a defensive stance.

"It's not that I don't like spending time with you; it just gets annoying when all you want to do is talk about Jess. We're together and I think that's where your focus should be, because even when I'm asking you about work or how you're doing, you always slick talking about her," he responded and he's telling the truth. Honestly, it's because I just want to know why her all the time and not me.

"I promise that I'm going to try and focus more on us, but I have to admit that I have been distracted with your friendship and I shouldn't have," I admitted.

"Why don't we get our grub on and then go back to the crib, so that I could show you just how much I love being in your presence," he flirted, causing me to smile.

I just want our relationship to go back to how it used to be, and if that means I need to stop stressing his friendship with Jess, so be it. I'm even willing to like her because she is a part of his life, so if I want a future with him, I'm going to have to accept her.

After dinner, we headed back to the house and I was ready to feel him inside of me, because his flirting had me horny as hell. I went into the bedroom and stripped out of my clothes, waiting on him to lock up because I wanted to get it popping. I don't even remember the last time that we even had any foreplay when having sex, so I wanted to remind him of what he's been missing.

He came upstairs and walked over to me, eyeing my body hungrily as he got down on his knees and devoured my pussy like he didn't just get finished eating. My right leg was slumped over his shoulder as I held onto his head with both hands, trying to manage my balance. My left leg gave me the stability I needed to fuck his face and when his stiff thick tongue dipped in and out of me, I lost it as my hips rotated against his mouth. My moans intensified into loud screams as I released all my juices into his mouth and I put my leg down, almost losing my balance from my legs shaking from the high I was on. He picked me up and carried me over to the bed, laying me on my back as he positioned himself between my legs, planting his big juicy lips on mine before sticking his tongue in my mouth, allowing me to taste my own juices.

"How that pussy taste?" he whispered in my ear, causing my pussy to jump.

I loved when he talked nasty to me because it always turned me on, sending hot sensations throughout my body.

"I'm more concerned with how that dick taste," I responded, helping him out of his jeans.

I wasn't big on sucking dick, but whatever I had to do to please my man; I was always willing to satisfy him like always. You would have thought that I swallowed the dick, the way I made his nine inches disappear into my mouth. He grabbed my hair as I deep throated his dick, hearing him hiss as if he was trying to control himself from cumming. So, I helped him out by removing his dick from my mouth, jerking it lightly with my hand and sucking his balls, causing him to curse me out in pleasure.

"Playtime over; it's time for me to punish that pussy," he said, tonguing me down before pushing me face down on the bed.

I got in position as I arched my back and hiked my ass up, ready for him to serve me what I been waiting for. This was his favorite position because he loved being in control, but I always held my own. I only tapped out one time and that was because I'd had too many drinks that night and he never let me live that down, even though I've been holding my own since.

"Tristian, oh my God, it feels so good," I cried out as he rammed his dick inside of me.

It hurt so good as I backed my ass up, meeting him stroke for stroke as I bit into my pillow, trying to suppress my screams. I knew he was on the verge of exploding, because he pulled me to the edge of the bed, holding onto my hips. When I tightened my pussy muscles, I felt that hot and tingly feeling that I get when I'm about to explode, so it was a wrap for both of us as we exploded together, leaving me in pure bliss. I crawled onto the bed, trying to catch my breath as he came behind me, wrapping his arms around my waist and resting his head on my shoulder.

"I love you and I'm sorry if I made you feel any different," he spoke into my ear.

"I love you too," I told him, feeling good that he finally said it without me saying it first.

I just hoped he meant everything he said, because I could really see myself spending the rest of my life with him if he allowed me to, I thought as I drifted off.

Chapter Eight
Trish

"Hey girl, I take it you got a call to be here too," I said to Jess once I saw her walk through my mother's front door.

"I sure did, so you know when Mama Bear calls, I'm here," she responded.

"I don't know what she's up to but your dad is here also, so I'm guessing that once Tristian gets here, the crazy lady will tell us why we're here. I bet it has something to do with you and Tristian's big head not speaking last month," I said.

"I doubt that she wouldn't say anything about that now, being that we been good for a minute now," she disagreed.

"Well, time will tell," I said as we both walked into the kitchen.

"Hey, Mama Bear," she spoke to my mom, giving her a hug. "Dad, what are you doing here?" she asked him.

"Last time I checked, I'm grown, baby girl," he said, grabbing her in a playful headlock, pretending to give her a noogie and causing her to laugh.

I heard the front door open, so I knew big-head Tristian had arrived; we all went to the family room and he wasn't alone. This wouldn't be the first time Toni's been to the house; I just didn't expect him to bring her when Mom wanted to talk to us about something. I didn't say anything because I guess he took my talk with him to heart, to start including her, so I spoke to her and kept it moving to the family room. I waited to see if she and Jess were going to speak to each other and when they did, all I could do was smile, believing that I had something to do with everyone trying to get along.

"Ok, so why are we here Mom Dukes?" Tristian asked, giving my mom a hug and Troy dap, before sitting his narrow ass down.

"So, you guys know that I have never been the type to beat around the bush, so I'm going to just tell you why your presence was requested. Trish and Tristian, you both know how hard it's been on me losing your father. I've come a long way since his death and that has a lot to do with Troy being here for me. He's been that void that I've been missing and although I feel that no man could ever replace your dad and

63

how I felt about him, that's not what this is. Jess, you have always held a special place in my heart since I first met you when you were just three years old.

I love you and always considered you to be another one of my children, so we would love to have you guys' blessing because we want to get married," my mom finished, nervously rubbing her hands together, waiting on a response from us.

"They can't be serious right now," I said to Jess and Tristian.

"I don't believe the two of you," Tristian said.

"Now look, don't…" Troy attempted, but Jess cut him off.

"It only took you guys like forever to say something; we knew that you guys were dating or whatever you want to call it. Dad, when I was fifteen, I came home early from school because I got a visit from Mother Nature and ruined my pants, so I had to leave school. I had no idea that you were going to be home, but you were and you weren't alone. I saw you and Mama Bear, but you guys didn't see me. I told Trish and Tristian what I saw and we waited for years for you or Mama Bear to say something," Jess let them know and Tristian and I co-signed that we knew.

"Mom, we're really happy for you guys, so again, about time and congrats," I said to her with tears in my eyes.

"Trish, don't you dare cry, because you know you're going to have all of us in here crying." My mom laughed, because she knew that I cried at the drop of a dime.

I couldn't help it because my mother deserved to be happy, as well as Troy, because they been through so much. They'd both loved and lost, so I'm just happy that they leaned on each other and I must say that it's a beautiful thing, and I wished they would have just told us sooner. They had us around here pretending like we didn't know, and Jess wanted to say something a long time ago, but I told her no.

"Ok, so since we're bearing good news and congrats, let me get in on it. Toni and I are having a baby and she's only four weeks, but I'm going to be a father," Tristian announced, wearing the happiest, silliest smile on his face.

"Oh my God, my baby is having a baby." my mom squealed.

We all offered our sentiments and although Jess said congrats, her eyes said something else. She was adamant about my big head brother being like a brother to her, but that look she's sporting; I wasn't so sure. Tristian and Toni stayed for about an hour before leaving, so it was just me and Jess kicking it in the family room.

"You good?" I asked her.

"I'm good; I'm happy for our parents, because they deserve to be happy again," she said.

"I'm not talking about them. I'm talking about Tristian having a baby with Toni." I twisted my lips, giving her the side eye because she knew exactly what I was talking about.

"Why wouldn't I be ok about that?" she spat, letting me know exactly what I ~~was~~ thought she was feeling to be correct.

"I told your ass about snapping at me, saying you were good would have sufficed." I mushed her ass.

"I snapped because you be reaching, after I told you Tristian is like a brother to me." She tried it, but I wasn't buying what she was selling.

"Ok, I'm going to let you have that because I love your ass. I was just thinking that maybe mother and son, and daddy and daughter could have a double wedding," I shot at her, but ran from the family room because she was good for throwing shit.

I spent the rest of my night talking to Mekhi on the phone and he was still stressing me about moving out of my mom's house to live with him. I still lived with my mother, because I just couldn't find it in my heart to leave her alone after my father passed. I was thinking, now that she and Troy came out of the closet about their relationship, maybe I could move out but I still didn't know if it would be with Mekhi. His baby mama is already giving him a tough time because he's in a relationship with me, so imagine if I moved in with him. She probably would never let him see his daughter, who he loves so much. He and I both are about sick of her and the games she's playing.

After getting off the phone with him, promising that I would think about moving in with him, I went upstairs to take a shower. Once my shower was done, for some reason I wasn't sleepy so I decided to watch television, but I didn't know what I wanted to watch. I started to think that maybe moving in with Mekhi wouldn't be a bad idea, because this isn't the first time at night that I just felt so lonely. My mom left with Troy and most likely, this is going to become an occurring thing for the two of them, so it was time for me to get my life and be with my man too.

Chapter Nine
Demayo

"Who is she, Kylief?" I barked in his face.

Kylief has been playing me to the curb for the last few months and I was sick of it, and I knew it had to be because of another bitch. I finally got him to agree to meet me at the Marriott, thinking that he finally decided to start treating me how he'd treated me in the beginning, but that was far from the case. He just hit it and now was trying to leave, talking about he has business to handle and I wasn't having it, because he was on some bullshit right now.

"You always on some drama shit and I don't have time for it, so like I said, I have business to handle. If anything, you should be thankful that I stopped by to give you a courtesy fuck, but no; that's not good enough for your crazy ass."

"Wow, are you really serious right now? So, suddenly, I'm a courtesy fuck, when did this happen?" I needed to know; I was on the verge of tears because I thought that we were more than fuck buddies.

"Why the fuck you standing here on some delusional shit, when you know that you are no longer my girl? Whenever we hook up it's for me to smash, so I'm going to need you to get the fuck out of my face, asking questions that don't concern you," he barked.

"If another bitch is involved, it does concern me because that means you just wasted a year of my fucking life. So, I was a smash buddy for a fucking year, Kylief?" I cried, getting in his face.

"Let me get the fuck up out of here, before you get on your Alex Forrest shit and I have to Dan Gallagher your ass," he said, referring to the characters from the movie, *Fatal Attraction*.

I didn't find his ass funny and yes, I get crazy sometimes but only when I'm being ignored or my feelings are being treated like they don't matter. I tried to control my breathing and my fist that balled as I watched him get dressed to leave and I swear it took everything in me not to put hands on him. I knew if I put my hands on him he would have made good on his threat and choked my ass to death. I needed to find out why this sudden change toward me occurred but my gut was telling me that it was another woman so I was going to find out.

"Demayo, lose my fucking number," he spoke. It bothered me that it was so easy for him to say that when the cum between my legs wasn't even dry yet, making me feel like a trick that he could just dismiss.

"Fuck you, Kylief," I yelled at his back as he exited the hotel room.

I sat on the hotel bed, letting my angry tears fall when my phone rang and it was Toni, but I let her call go to voicemail. I didn't want or need to hear about how happy she and Tristian were and the baby that she was having, when my shit was falling apart. I always told her that she should have left Tristian because if it was me, I would never allow my man to do half the things that he was doing, but I was being treated just as bad as she was. So, damn right I didn't want to hear about how Tristian got his act together since she got pregnant, and how she hopes it leads to her being his wife. I knew that once I got back to work at the bank, I was going to have no choice but to hear it, so I guess I'll just wait until then but for now; I wasn't taking any of her calls.

I waited for about twenty minutes after Kylief left, before I decided to go to the bowling alley to see if that's where he went, being that he said he had business to handle. His bowling alley was the only business I was aware of, so when he wasn't there; I drove to his home in Ridgewood and his black Lexus that he drove to the hotel was parked out front. I pulled around the block and parked a few houses down and just waited. I knew that he had to be seeing someone else and I was going to find out who this bitch was. She wasn't about to take what belonged to me, because I have invested too much time in his ass. Kylief emerged from his house like forty-five minutes later, looking fresh out the shower and dressed like the thug that I loved to hate, but couldn't for the life of me. He's so damn handsome with that bad boy image; I just couldn't leave him alone and now he's just dumped me for the second time, like I meant nothing to him. Kylief is a successful businessman, so I know that he has women coming at him from all angles and if he acted on any; I didn't know because he never gave me a reason to think that he did until now. He's trying to convince me that my few outbursts that were triggered because of him are the reason he didn't want to be with me anymore, but his reasoning had "new bitch" written all over it.

I followed him all the way to Gateway Mall in Brooklyn and when he pulled up to the Red Lobster, I knew that he was meeting with whoever this new female is he's been seeing, so I sat and waited. He sat in his car as well, so I'm assuming he was waiting for her to pull up and I felt my emotions trying to get the best of me, and I prayed that God gave me the strength to stay seated in my car. I rested my head on the steering wheel briefly, trying my best to stay calm but calm went out the window when I lifted my head and saw that Kylief was opening the door of a car that was very familiar. The car belonged to Jess; it was confirmed when she stepped out of the car and his hand caressed the small of her back, which caused me to lose it. So, now that Tristian wasn't fucking with her like that, she thought that she was going to fuck with my man now.

I jumped out of my car and with them being so busy admiring each other, they didn't see me coming. I walked right up on them and grabbed Jess by the pink hoodie she was wearing, pulling her down to the ground, attempting to beat her senseless. She blocked her face as I kept pounding, until I was pulled up by my weave and flung to the ground. Feeling dazed from hitting the ground, she was now giving me the same ass whopping that I was just giving her. I tried blocking her blows, but she was raining them down on me rather quickly, so I just kept my face covered to keep from getting hit. Kylief finally pulled her off of me, but not before she kicked me in my mouth, drawing blood. At that point, I just knew that he was going to help me up, but instead, he was making sure that she was good. It crushed me that he didn't even care that my shit was leaking and that I was still on the ground in pain.

"So, you're really not going to help me up?" I cried.

"Fuck you, bitch," he spoke with venom in his voice, before spitting on me like I was trash.

"I swear I could kill that bitch right now. Who the fuck is this hoe and why did she just attack me?" I heard her ask him.

"Get in your car and follow me," he told her, opening her car door and once she was in, he walked to his car and pulled out.

A few people came to assist me, but I told them to get the fuck away from me, triggering nasty comments from a few. I heard someone say that I deserved that ass whooping. Another one was saying, "When will these young girls learn to stop fighting over men that don't give a shit about them?"

I was embarrassed and my feelings were hurt as I limped to my car thinking that maybe those people were right. I moaned out in pain as I got into my car, because my side was killing me and my tooth felt loose from the kick to my mouth, and I swear she was going to pay for that shit.

I'm pissed that I allowed myself to fall in love with Kylief's ass because clearly, the feelings weren't mutual. I felt dumb as hell as I pulled out of the parking lot, taking my ass home where I should have gone, instead of following him to begin with.

Chapter Ten
Jess

My hands were shaking as I gripped the steering wheel, because that's how fucking mad I was right now. I didn't sign up for this shit to be fighting in the street with some bitch that I didn't even know so if this is what Kylief had going on I wanted no parts of it. I followed him to what I'm assuming to be his place of residence and I couldn't wait to get inside to find out what the fuck was going on. He parked in the driveway and although it was a two-car garage, I opted out of pulling up in his driveway because I wasn't sure if I would be staying long, depending on what came out of his mouth.

"Why are you parking on the street?" he inquired but I ignored him, walking towards the house.

"Do you want to tell me why that bitch attacked me?" I barked.

"Listen, I have no control over what that bitch did, but I do apologize for her actions," he said and I looked at him like he was crazy, because he was going to have to come better than that.

He just had me fighting in the street like I'm not grown and haven't been out of high school for five years, so yes, he was going to need to come better than that shit he just spat out of his mouth.

"I'm not blaming you for her actions, but what I'm asking you is, what was the cause of her actions? We could start off with who the fuck is she?" I sneered at him.

"She's someone that I was seeing before I started seeing you and as you can see, she didn't take it well. She had no right putting her hands on you and I'm sure after that ass whooping you gave her, she'll think twice about trying you again," he chuckled, finding humor in what he just said but I didn't.

"I don't do drama unless it's drama that I caused, so if this is going to be a reoccurring action from her, I think it would be safe for me to cut all ties now," I said seriously, because I was too fucking classy and pretty to be street fighting with anyone.

I haven't had a fight in my twenty-four years of living and I wasn't about to start now behind any man. I don't care how much I like him; it's just not going to happen and if she feels the need to keep trying to fight for a man that doesn't want her anymore, she will have to take it to the next female, because it will not be this chick right here.

"I promise you that you will not have any other issues with her, and again, I'm sorry for that shit back at the restaurant." He tried to convince me, but how could he be sure that she wouldn't come for me again? If he had some control she would have known not to even approach me.

I asked if I could use the restroom so that I could check my face; I knew that I had a few scratches because my face was stinging. Once in the bathroom, I looked in the mirror and the damage wasn't too bad, besides a little bruising under my eyes and a few scratches on my left cheek. Once I walked back downstairs, I started to look around and I had to say that his home was beautiful, but I was still pissed so I wasn't going to tell him that I admired his home. I went to take a seat on the sofa but as soon as he heard my footsteps, he called me to the kitchen where he was at. He was seasoning chicken breasts when I walked in, so I'm assuming he was going to try and make up for his ex-chick ruining dinner for us both. I took a seat at the kitchen island and just watched him work his way around the kitchen and to my surprise, he was doing a hell of a job with his finished project looking just as good as any restaurant I've been to.

He made chicken parmesan with spaghetti and garlic bread that looked and smelled good. He put a bottle of Moët Rosé on the table and I was ready to dig in and down a few glasses. Hopefully, it would put me in a better mood because I was still pissed at his ass.

Kylief was staring at how fast I was eating, but I could give two shits; I was going in on this food because this nigga did that. I was licking my fingers and the whole nine, because it was no shame in my game.

"How does it taste?" He laughed at me licking my fingers.

"You got some skills, so I'm enjoying it," I said, picking up my napkin and wiping my mouth.

"I wasn't going to show you my cooking skills until later in the relationship, but I needed to get back on your good side after what went down," he said.

"I'm good over here, because I already expressed how I felt and what I expected from this situation," I told him, going back to eating my food.

"I got you," was all he said as he got busy on his plate.

After dinner, I was feeling a little tipsy, so I felt the need to try and ask some of the questions that I probably wouldn't have asked otherwise.

"So, who was that female that can't seem to let go and how long were you with her?" I asked.

"Her name is Demayo and I was seeing her for about a year."

"What kind of name is Demayo and what happened that you didn't want to see her any more?" I wanted to know.

"I have no idea what kind of name it is, being her mama gave her the name and I ended it because she was getting possessive. But enough about her; I'm more interested in spending my time with you and not talk about someone who means nothing to me," he said, pulling me toward him.

He smelled so good as I rested my face into his chest, just taking him all in as I felt my panties getting moist from just being in his presence. We have yet to take it to the next level, so I was wondering if tonight would be the night being that I was feeling bold tonight.

He kissed me on my lips and I wasted no time tonguing him down and his tongue felt so good in my mouth. I couldn't help but savor the taste from the wine that lingered on his

79

tongue as I dry humped his leg. I opened my eyes briefly and jumped out of his arms, causing him to look at me crazy.

"S-s-someone was looking through the window," I stuttered.

He rushed to the door, but not before grabbing a gun from his waist that I didn't even know was there. He swung the front door open and that's when we both heard tires screech as the person hauled ass down the street. He was outside, but I had no idea what or who he was looking for when we both heard whoever it was speed off. But, what I did know was that I was ready to go home. I'm not going to lie and say that I wasn't shaken up by what just happened and I wasn't about to get caught up in whatever he had going on.

"I'm going to head home," I said to him when he finally came back into the house.

"You don't have to go, Jess, I'm sure it was nothing," he had the nerve to say.

"So, someone looking through your window is nothing," I asked being sarcastic, which he picked up on, because he took a deep breath before speaking.

"Look, I didn't mean it like that, Jess, all I'm saying is that you don't have to go, because I'm not going to let anything happen to you," he cleared up.

"I don't doubt that your able to protect me, but I'm concerned with why would anyone be looking through your window watching us."

"I honestly don't have the answer as to who would be doing some sick shit like that, but I promise you that you're safe here," he tried to convince me.

I really didn't want to leave, but my nerves were shot and all I was going to do was keep worrying myself if I stayed. But after thinking about it, I'd been waiting to spend some alone time with him, so I decided that I would stay.

"Ok, if I stay, I swear you better protect me with your life," I said seriously.

"I wouldn't have it any other way, now bring your fine ass over here so that we could watch a movie," he said.

"First, I'm going to need you to draw all of the curtains and make sure all of the doors are locked," I told him, because I needed to feel safe.

I wanted to ask him so bad if he thought that it might have been the female from earlier, but decided to leave it alone for now. He put the movie *Sleepless* into the DVD player, so I got comfortable in his arms as we watched the movie. He was enjoying it, but I wasn't liking it too much. It was just too much going on in the movie, which was a bit confusing to me and I expected a better performance from Jamie Foxx. I don't know when I dozed off, but when I woke up, he was sleeping with his head back against the sofa, so I tapped him lightly to let him know that I was going to head out. He tried to talk me into staying the night, but I had to be to work in the morning so I had to decline, but I told him that I would stay with him another night.

Chapter Eleven
Jess

I felt like I was being followed on my way to work this morning, but I chalked it up to my still being shook about last night. Shaking my head at my being paranoid, I pulled up in the parking lot at work, just as my phone alerted me that I had a text message. I was early as usual, so I sat in the car to see who it was and it was Tristian, who I haven't spoken to in a minute.

Tristian- I miss you. What are you getting into later?

Me- I miss you too, Mr. I don't have time for Jess anymore.

Tristian- I know I been missing in action, that's why I'm hitting you up.

Me- Well, I have no plans after work so what did you have in mind?

Tristian- We could get something to eat to catch up.

Me- Ok, I'm down, just hit me up before I get off work and let me know where to meet you.

Tristian- Cool. Later.

I was on my way to meet Tristian at the Blue Ribbon Sushi Bar & Grill, and I never understood why he liked eating at that damn expensive restaurant. I was being treated, so I was just going with the flow and like I told him earlier, I missed him, so I would have met him at the dog park. He was standing against his car when I pulled up, so I parked and got out so that we could go inside to eat.

"Hey, you," he greeted me with a hug, towering over me.

"Hey stranger," I said playfully, punching him in his arm.

Once inside and we were seated, I started looking at the menu because for some reason, our friendship now seemed forced.

"Do you know what you're ordering?" he asked me, I guess trying to make conversation.

"I don't know yet, being they so damn expensive," I told him.

"Jess, you don't have to worry about prices, I got you," he assured me.

I ordered a house salad with the grilled half-chicken and Tristian decided on the sushi bar salad with the Atlantic salmon and we both had the sake cocktail.

"So, now that we got that out of the way, what's been going on with you?" he asked.

"Nothing much, besides my having to beat Kylief's ex-girlfriend's ass the other day," I vented.

"Are you serious? What happened?" he asked.

"I don't know; he invited me to dinner and when I pulled up, she came out of nowhere and attacked me. He says that she's bitter because he doesn't want to be with her, but that shit pissed me off. You know I never had a fight in my life, so I was thrown off, but I ended up beating her ass."

"So, he just let the two of you fight over him?"

"Well, she was fighting over him; I was just defending myself, but he did break it up." I felt the need to defend Kylief.

"Are you sure he not still messing with her?" he questioned.

"I don't know if he is or if he isn't, but he says that he broke it off so until I see different, I have no choice but to take his word."

"That nigga better treat you the way you deserve to be treated or he's going to have to see me," he said and he wasn't joking.

"I'm good, but enough about me, how are things going with you and Toni, now that she's carrying your baby?" I wanted to know.

"We good, she's just clingier now so I've been going to the shop making sure to go straight to the crib after work."

"Clingier then before, how is that humanly possible?" We laughed.

"Jess, I just want to apologize for how I came at you, and I just want our friendship to go back to how it used to be," he offered.

"I know you're sorry, that's why I forgave you. But seriously, I know that you were just looking out for me," I said to him, even though I wanted to tell him that he was acting like a jealous boyfriend.

I watched as he looked at his phone and I couldn't help but to laugh, because this was a record for Toni. It took her an entire hour before he was supposed to be home from work to hit his phone, so I found it hilarious. He looked over at me with a smirk on his face, so I told him to go ahead and give her a call to let her know he was on his way, being we were just about done with dinner.

"Thanks for dinner, now get home before she activates that locator on your phone," I joked.

"You're standing here laughing, but her ass probably does have a tracker on my damn phone," he said seriously before giving me a hug, telling me to get home safe.

I got in my car and once again I got that eerie feeling, but I brushed it off as I blew my horn at him, pulling out. Pulling up to my house, my phone rang and it was Kylief so I answered the call, balancing the phone on my shoulder as I grabbed my bag and locked my car door.

"Hey, what's up? I haven't spoken to you all day," he said into the phone, but I didn't get a chance to answer him as I screamed out in pain, causing the phone to fall.

Somebody came from behind me and hit me in the back of my head with something dazing me and I tried to fight the person off but I was too dazed. I was hit a few more times in the head as I fell to the ground. Trying to get up, I felt dizzy, falling back to the ground before everything went black.

I opened my eyes and immediately, my hand went to my forehead, because of the excruciating pain I was feeling from my head. The light and the noise from whatever machine that they had monitoring me was pain alone as it annoyed the hell out of me. I knew that I was in the hospital but I tried to figure out how the hell I got here, because I remember getting hit and falling to the ground, but I don't remember anybody there to help me.

"Are you ok, baby?" I heard Mama Bear's voice and that's when I noticed that my father, Tristian and Trish was in the room.

"My head hurts," I moaned out in pain.

"Let me tell the nurse that you need something stronger, because you're still in pain," she said, rubbing my hand before walking away.

My dad looked like he'd been crying and I understood what he was feeling, because I'm his baby girl, so it had to be hard knowing someone tried to hurt me. Tristian's facial expression told me that he was pissed off and probably ready to go to war with whoever was responsible. He was the laid-back, always joking type, but when you fuck with someone he cares about, he becomes a savage.

I don't know who would do something like this to me and to be honest, the only person that comes to mind would be

Demayo, being she was the only person I had a confrontation with recently. I would hope that this was a robbery attempt and that she wouldn't go this far over a man that didn't want anything to do with her anymore. I wasn't trying to lose my life behind some dick, whether that dick wanted me or not, because it just wasn't that serious for me.

"Do you think that this has anything to do with the fight you had with dude's ex?" Trish asked, causing me to roll my eyes.

She knew that she shouldn't have said that, because now my father really was going to worry, knowing someone purposely tried to harm me.

"What fight?" my dad asked and I could see his jaw tighten.

"Can we talk about this later, or at least when she's feeling better?" Mama Bear said, coming to my rescue.

"I'll wait until she's feeling better, but I want to hear about this fight and who the hell this man is that you're seeing. If he's bringing harm to my baby girl, he's going to get dealt with," he said, sounding like an old gangsta and if my head wasn't banging, I'd be laughing right now.

Tristian remained stone-faced and didn't say anything, so I knew he was in his feelings and I wished that he wasn't here right now. Trish was trying to make eye contact with me so that she could apologize for her big ass mouth, but I avoided making eye contact with her "slip of the tongue ass" like always. She could never hold water. She knew that bringing up the fight was going to cause my dad to dislike Kylief, even though he never met him, but she couldn't help herself.

The doctor wanted to keep me for observation for another night. Everyone had already left the hospital, so I called Kylief to let him know what happened. He said that he was on his way and I quickly regretted making the call, because Tristian's ass walked back in the room. I had no idea that when he left earlier, he wasn't leaving with everyone else.

"You good?" I asked him.

"Shouldn't I be asking you that question?" he said like he was mad with me.

"What's wrong with you, Tristian?" I asked, trying not to get angry.

"No, I need you to tell me what the hell is wrong with you and why you don't leave this nigga alone because he's no good for you. You out here fighting and now somebody tries to hurt you behind this nigga, so clearly, he's not telling you the truth about his situation," he barked.

"Whoa, where the hell is all of this coming from, and how can you just assume that this has something to do with him? The police confirmed that my pocketbook wasn't at the scene, so clearly it had to be a robbery," I snapped.

"I don't give a fuck what the police reported. I know that you been living in that neighborhood for like forever and no shit never popped off. You get with this nigga, now shit happening to you and I swear if I have to see that nigga, I will," he cursed, just as Kylief walked into the room and all I could think was, *please don't let these two get into it.*

"How are you feeling?" Kylief asked, kissing me on my forehead without acknowledging Tristian, but that could have been because of the mean mug Tristian was giving him.

I closed my eyes and just prayed that Tristian would just let it go, being that we were in the hospital. Knowing Tristian, I'm going to have to page the nurse to get security. *Damn.*

Chapter Twelve
Tristian

"Kylief, this is my friend, Tristian, that I told you about," Jess said to this nigga.

I didn't need no fucking introduction when that nigga walked in here and didn't acknowledge a nigga. I don't know what this clown-ass dude did to Jess, but she was acting gullible and that shit was pissing me the fuck off. She knows she's never had any problems with anyone until his ass came into the picture, but she's going to sit in my face and downplay the shit like she's known his ass a long time.

"I'm good on this nigga, just remember what the fuck I said," I told her ass before leaving out of her room.

I sat outside my crib, getting my attitude in check before going inside because knowing Toni's ass, she was going to assume that it had to do with my being jealous of Jess' relationship. I needed to hook up with my boys outside of the shop because when I needed to vent, I always brought that shit to the work place. My ass will be walking around that bitch like a female on her period, getting clowned by my niggas because if nobody else knew, my boys knew how I felt about Jess. I didn't want to see Jess fall for this nigga and end up being hurt behind being blinded by love or some shit. I felt like I was calm enough to go inside, so I got out of the car and went inside the crib and Toni was sitting on the couch, talking on the phone. She ended her call once she saw me walking into the living room, but I wasn't sweating that shit because it probably wasn't nobody but her annoying ass co-worker that she's always talking about.

"How's Jess?" she asked and being she seemed genuinely concerned, I decided to answer her.

"She's ok, but the doctor kept her overnight for observation," I told her.

"Well, I'm glad that she's ok and I know you're ready to murder something and I don't blame you. I left your dinner covered inside of the microwave," she said, causing me to look around to make sure that I walked into the right house.

"Don't do that, I know Jess and I have our differences, but I would never enjoy seeing her hurt," she said and I believed her.

I went into the kitchen to warm up my plate and then went back to the living room to sit with Toni, who was now watching *Little Women Atlanta*. I didn't want to watch this ghetto show filled with little women but I decided to let it rock, since she complained about me not watching the shows that she likes, but I expect her to watch my shows.

"So how was your day and how is the little one?" I asked, having enough of watching this bullshit.

"My day was fine and I no longer have to stand all day, because my supervisor allows me to sit at the window now. The little one is doing fine and the morning sickness is finally getting better so that's a plus," she said, but still looking at the television.

"I'm going to head upstairs, so come join me when you finish watching your ratchet television for the night," I told her, ready to go up and shower and get in the bed.

I couldn't help but think about calling Jess to see if she was ok, but I didn't want her to think that I was calling to apologize. I meant everything that I said to her about that dude, so for that, I will not be apologizing. Just as I was about to go and get into the shower, my phone rang. *Speak of the devil herself.*

"Speak," I barked into the phone.

"So, that's how you answer your phone now?" she asked.

"That's how I'm answering it for your ass," I said into the phone as I removed my shirt, followed by my jeans.

"Anyway, what are you doing right now?" she inquired.

"I'm about to take a shower and get ready to hit the sheets. Why?"

"I was just asking, damn," she spat.

"Aren't you supposed to be getting some rest, Jess?"

"Yeah, but I wanted to call and tell you that what you did was rude as hell, when you don't even have the facts to what happened to me," she said causing my jaw to tighten, because if she was calling me to defend this nigga, we were going to have a problem.

"I have all the facts that I need and the number-one fact being that none of this shit was happening to you before meeting his ass. Are you sure that his only business is that fucking bowling alley? And now that I think about it, you did meet his ass at your job that house criminal attorneys," I reminded her ass.

"You're being so unfair right now, like you haven't known me all my life. Don't you think that if for a second I thought that this had something to do with him, that I wouldn't distant myself from him?" she sighed.

"I'm just calling the shit the way I see it, Jess, and if you don't understand that all I'm doing is looking out for you, I don't know what to tell you."

"How about you just trust that I know what I'm doing, just like I let you rock after I tried to warn you about all those tricks you were running with before Toni. I told you that those bitches didn't have your best interest at heart and what happened? They all cheated on your fucking ass, but did I get all bent out of shape when you told me to mind my business, Tristian?" she said, getting in her feelings.

"Look, I'm not trying to argue with you or get you upset, and if that's the nigga you want to be with, then I'm going to mind my business. All I'm going to say is be careful and make sure that the nigga is legit, because I will body his ass if I find out different," I repeated to her ass, letting her know how serious I was.

"I appreciate your concern, but I'm good."

"Ok, 'Ms. I'm Good', get some rest and I'll talk to you tomorrow," I told her.

"I love you," she sang into the phone.

"I love you too, Jess," I told her before ending the call.

It was becoming harder and harder to hide the feelings that I have for Jess, especially when she's seeing someone. The thought of someone touching her the way I have always wanted to touch her was killing me inside, making me want to murder that nigga. Jess always says that we were raised as brother and sister and for the life of me; I've been trying to get out of the brother-friend zone for a minute now, to no avail. I wanted her to understand that I really don't care about the way she perceives how we grew up; the fact remains that we aren't blood related.

She was acting like she wasn't crushing on me at one time and I just knew that was going to be our breaking point to explore, but she got scared and friend-zoned my ass again. Granted, we never had a "take it there" moment, but feelings have been expressed before, so nothing has changed my feelings for her. I decided to take my ass to the bathroom to take a shower and stop stressing the shit that I had no control over.

"Hey, you good? I'm sorry that I wasn't more attentive towards you when you got home," Toni said, approaching me as I was coming out of the bathroom.

She stepped on her tippy toes to kiss my lips as she caressed my dick through my towel, letting me know that she wanted to get it popping and I was game. I needed the distraction from what my mind had going on as far as Jess and her new man. I sometimes ask myself why I just wasn't content with Toni, knowing that I do love her and there was no doubt that I wasn't attracted to her fine ass. She stood at 5'6", 154 pounds, had a brown sugar skin tone, hazel eyes that matched her skin tone, with a body that was banging.

She must have realized that my mind drifted again, because she removed my towel taking my dick into her mouth, causing me to groan in pleasure as I held on to her braids, pumping in and out of her mouth. I grunted once she started sucking on my balls, because I wasn't ready to bust just yet. As much as I wanted her to continue, I knew that I had to stop her because like I said I wasn't ready to bust yet. I helped her up off her knees, pulling her Mickey Mouse printed nightshirt over her head, revealing that she wasn't wearing anything under it. I massaged her ass with one hand, while I played in her pussy with the other from behind, causing her to moan out in pleasure. I was ready to feel that pregnant pussy again, so I bent her ass over the edge of the bed and plunged into the pussy, hitting her with deep long strokes as she gyrated her hips, fucking me stroke for stroke. Her pussy was so wet, it sounded like I was stirring a pot of grits that was boiling and popping at the same time.

"Fuck this pussy," she screamed, so I did just that, fucking her so hard that when we both finally came she passed out. I was minutes behind her, pulling her into my arms as I took my ass to sleep.

Chapter Thirteen
Jess

I've been home from the hospital for a few days and feeling better so I was chilling at Mama Bear's house with Trish. The doctor said that I didn't suffer from a concussion and that the headaches should cease, but if they didn't, for me to make an appointment with my primary doctor. I have since cancelled all my credit cards and ordered new identification, as well as having all my locks changed. It was better to be safe than sorry and even if I wasn't going to play it safe, my dad was on my ass about it. He was still upset and what pissed me off just a little is that he was pissed at Kylief, the same as everyone else, like New York wasn't known for grimy ass motherfuckers taking what didn't belong to them. But no, they rather blame him.

"So, you told me that Kylief is upset with you, but you didn't tell me why," Trish interrupted my thoughts with her "always being thirsty for the tea" self.

"I didn't know that when everyone left my hospital room that Tristian was going to come back, so I had already called Kylief and when he said he was on his way, I told him ok. If I knew that Tristian didn't leave, I would have told Kylief not to come, because Tristian always tripping. So, when Kylief came through, your brother being in his feelings like always, was rude and Kylief just felt that I should have said something. I got upset because even if Tristian didn't walk out of the room after being rude, I just felt that if Kylief felt some way about it, he should have checked Tristian and not check me after he already left," I stressed to her.

"Jess, I know you, so don't go getting defensive for what I'm about to say," she said, so I kept my mouth shut, waiting for her to speak on it.

"You have to admit that nothing like this has ever happened to you until you started messing with him and I'm not saying that it's because of him. It just seems that way, so that's why everyone is in an uproar about it and you can't really blame them for it. You're my friend and I love you and all I ask is that you be careful, because you really don't know much about him, besides he owns the bowling alley," she finished.

She was right when she said she knows me, because I did take a defensive stance about what she just said, but decided to take a deep breath before responding.

"Trish, I could say some things about you and Mekhi, because you been seeing him for eight months and I've never met him. All you do is spin stories about him and his baby mama, but does he even exist?" I took it there.

I know I just said I was going to take a deep breath before responding, but what could I say I wouldn't be me if I didn't clap back and call her out on her shit.

"Are you serious, Jess? I haven't introduced him yet, because I just want to make sure that he's the one this time, before bringing him around my family," she spat, knowing she didn't believe that shit she just said herself.

"Well, whatever your reason, it still doesn't justify why I haven't met him yet, being that I met all the other busters you dated."

"Jess, why are you making this about me, when we're talking about your man?" she barked, snaking her neck and I knew she was in her feelings.

"We were talking about my man, but now we're talking about your man. I've been quiet going with the flow, but fuck that since everyone has an opinion about my dude. I've met all your boyfriends within the first week, so what's so different about this one? Is he ugly? In a wheelchair? Or maybe it's because he has one eye," I said, causing her to laugh.

"Girl, you ain't shit and if you want to meet Mekhi, then let's do a double-date so that I can meet this man that got you coming for me," she said, rolling her eyes.

"I wasn't coming for you. I'm just trying to make you understand that blaming him for my being robbed is unfair, unless you have facts," I told her.

"You're right, so his ass is innocent until proven guilty I guess," she said, giving me the side eye, causing me to shake my head at her ass.

"I'm about to get up out of here because my pressure is up and my head's starting to hurt, fucking with you but I'll call you later. I'll set up that double date so don't try and back out because then I'm really going to believe that he doesn't exist," I told her ass as I got ready to go.

I left my pain medication at home so I needed to bounce and get my fix, because if I go too long without the medication, it doesn't work once I take it. Once I got home, I made sure to be aware of my surroundings as I made my way to my front door. I nervously dug into my bag for my keys and cursed myself for not taking them out before exiting the car. I used to keep my house keys on the same ring as the car keys, but after losing my car keys before not only was I stuck, I couldn't get into my place either. As soon as I got inside, I locked the door thankful that I got inside without being attacked again, and I hated that I was going to always think that something was going to happen to me coming or leaving home.

I took two of my pain pills before taking a shower, because Kylief was coming over so that we could talk, so I wanted to be washed and be headache free before he got here. After my shower, I put on a pair of pajama pants and a sports bra before picking up my phone to send Kylief a text to see what time he was going to be here. He said that he was about five minutes away, so I rushed into the bathroom to brush my teeth and to check my hair in the mirror, before heading downstairs to wait on him. He had the butterflies in my stomach floating, even though I was still upset with him and I knew that had to do with me starting to fall for him. I think that's the reason I refuse to believe that all my misfortune was because of him. Tristian made a point about how I met him and although I hated to pry, I needed to know why he was there at the office the morning of the day I met him. I heard the knock on the door so I rushed over, looking through the peephole before letting him inside and when I saw the bag in his hand, I knew he was blessing me with some wings, which gave him an automatic pass to cease my attitude.

"I see you showing off those tight ass abs," he smirked, licking his lips.

"Yep my tight abs, fat ass, double-D's all on display, so be sure to look and don't touch, because your ass is on punishment." I smirked, licking my lips and mocking his ass causing him to laugh.

"So, I guess I better leave since I'm on punishment and my wings are going with me," he threatened, pretending like he was going to leave.

"If you walk out of that door with my wings, punishment is going to be the least of your worries." We laughed as I took the bag out of his hand.

"What?" I asked, looking up from eating my wings.

"I'm just saying, you must be feeling a nigga because every time you eat now, you be smacking your lips and licking your fingers. But on that first date at the bowling alley, your ass was eating the wings with a fork," he said, causing me to burst out laughing because I didn't even realize that I was doing any of that this time.

He has to understand that these wings are so damn good that I didn't have time to worry about him sitting across from me watching me.

"Well, I don't know about feeling you, but what I will say is that you know how good these wings are, so that's my story and I'm sticking to it," I smiled, going back in on my wings.

"Stop fronting; you know you feeling me but don't sweat it because I'm feeling you too," he said, moving closer to me and sucking the jerk seasoning from my lips.

"Eww, you so nasty," I told him, pushing him playfully before wiping my mouth with a napkin.

"Trust me, that's nothing compared to how nasty I could get," he flirted, giving me hot flashes at the thought of how nasty he could get.

I was stuck on stupid for a minute as I couldn't find any words right now, because he was now caressing my breast. As good as his hands felt on my breast, I was not about to be fucking on my sofa, so I stood pulling him with me as we ascended the stairs. Once in my bedroom, we wasted no time getting undressed and I found myself on my knees as he stood before me. I held onto his dick, admiring the length and thickness that caused my mouth to water just a little. I watched as the veins in his dick pulsated as he anticipated me taking him into my mouth, with me deciding to put him out of his misery. I took him in as deep as my mouth would allow as he put his hands behind his head, taking in my skills as he pumped in and out of my mouth. I grabbed his ass as I bobbed my head up and down, using my mouth as a suction cup as I pulled all his cum up out of him.

"Damn girl," he panted, pulling me towards him.

Now it was his turn to pleasure me and my knees buckled before his lips even made contact, causing him to smirk. I was nervous and just like he was anticipating my mouth, I was anticipating what that tongue was about to do. When he turned me around with my backside facing him, pushing me down as he stuck his tongue in my ass, I lost it. He was penetrating me with his tongue, causing me to bite down, trying to control the scream of pleasure that was dying to be released. I held onto the sheet for dear life as his tongue traveled to my slit, dipping his tongue in and out of me.

"Oh, shit, I'm about to cum," I squealed, bucking wildly as I released my juices in his mouth.

Kylief didn't even give me a chance to catch my breath before entering me from behind, hitting my G-spot with long, deep strokes. My body rocked with each stroke and I swear it felt good, so good that I had tears falling from my eyes. I never felt this kind of pleasure before and he had my emotions all over the place.

"Back that ass up for me," he whispered in my ear, biting on it lightly before sucking on it, causing another release.

"That's right, cum on this dick, but I'm not done with that ass yet," he spoke in a cocky tone and I just knew he was wearing that smirk of his when he said it.

He pulled out of me, pulling me with him as he took a seat on the loveseat in the corner of my room. He pulled me onto his lap, entering me again, causing me to gasp at trying to take his length in this position. I put my hands on his shoulders and lifted my butt, slowly at first, until I felt comfortable enough to ride him without doing damage to my insides. He grabbed my hips, pumping inside of me slowly, getting me comfortable with his length in this position and once I started to feel pleasure, I rode his dick like I was going for first place at the races. We fucked until the sun started to rise and a bitch was worn out with a sore pussy, *but it was well worth it*, I thought as I fell asleep in his arms.

Chapter Fourteen
Jess

Kylief and I have been dating for a little over five months and he was starting to become possessive. I started noticing a change in his behavior, which started with him being controlling after the first time we had sex. Things that never bothered him before was suddenly a problem for him, like he always told me that he loved how I dressed when I went to work. Now, all I hear is that my slacks are too tight and I was wearing them to entice the men that frequent the office, the same as I did him. He also knows that if he wants to text me at work all day, we could do that without a problem, but he knows that I can't sit and talk to him on the phone and he never had a problem with it until now. My boss had a meeting the other day and needed me to sit in and take some notes because his assistant was out for the day, so my phone had to stay at my desk. When I got back to my desk, I had like ten disrespectful messages and like twenty missed calls, basically accusing me of not being at work and with some nigga. I called Trish up and she was meeting me after work to grab a few drinks, because I needed to tell her what was going on because I needed some advice. I've never experienced anything like this before and I honestly didn't know what to do.

Damn he was ringing my phone again, but I just let it go to voicemail because I didn't feel like giving him a rundown of my day. He always demanded that I give him a play by play and always wanted to know if anybody tried to push up on me and it was becoming aggravating. I'm not going to lie; the first few times he did it, I was kind of flattered that he cared to even ask if someone was trying to talk to me. I mean, the jealousy act looked good on him, but now it wasn't cute to me anymore and like I said, I needed some advice on how to get him to understand that it wasn't flattering anymore. It got so bad that I had to take the location off my phone because he showed up at the library one day and I know for a fact that I didn't tell him that I was going to be there, because it was a last-minute decision. When we first met, he claimed to be so busy and that he didn't have much time being he was a businessman, but that shit changed too and now he always wanted to be in my presence.

When I got to the bar, Trish was standing out front, so we walked in together and took a seat so that I could let her know what was going on. I just hoped that she wasn't going to be judgmental and just give me some advice on how to deal with how Kylief went from perfect to possessive.

"Hey, girl thanks for coming," I said, giving her a hug.

"No problem, just tell me what's going on because you didn't sound like yourself," she stressed.

"Honestly, I don't know what's going on, but it seems that Kylief is showing a side of him now that we're together that I didn't see in the beginning.. I tell you no lie, the day after our first time having sex, he just changed up on me; it started out with things that I honestly thought was cute until now," I said, trying to fight my tears of frustration of the situation I put myself in.

"So, what kind of things is he doing?" she asked and I could tell that she was getting pissed already.

"He's being possessive, controlling and he showed up to the library last week, letting me know that he must have a tracking device on my phone. I turned the location off on my phone because I know that I didn't tell him that I was going to be there. Oh, and the other day my boss asked me to sit in a meeting, because his assistant was out for the day and when I returned to my desk, I had like ten text messages and twenty missed calls. He was basically accusing me of not being at work and being with another man, and stressed what he was going to do to me if he found out that I was with another man."

"I think that you should leave him alone and let Tristian or your dad know what's going on before his ass hurts you," she said, but that wasn't the advice that I really wanted, because I didn't think that he would do anything to me.

"I'm just going to tell him that I think it's best that we go our separate ways like, give each other some space and leave it at that, because I don't want Tristian approaching him. I just hate that he made me fall in love with his ass, just to treat me like his property. I have never fallen for anyone this quickly; he just seemed like the man I been waiting for," I said sadly.

"Fuck that and I swear, if he puts his fucking hands on you, I'll kill his ass. Jess, break it off with him and if you need me there when you do it, I don't have a problem being there," she said seriously.

"Jess, I know how you feel about him but I never trusted him, especially after meeting him that first time. Something about him just rubbed me the wrong way and I didn't tell you this, but Mekhi said when we went to the bathroom, Kylief accused him of looking at your ass. He said that Kylief threatened him in a joking manner, but he didn't think that he was joking. Mekhi said his head never turned in our direction when we got up to use the bathroom, and that he would never disrespect me by looking at my best friend's ass," she told me and I believed her, because he sees shit that nobody else sees or has even done for him to see.

He claimed the waiter at the restaurant touched my hand when he was asking me about my order and it never happened. He cursed the waiter out so bad and threatened to take his life and I swear, I was so fucking embarrassed because that man was just doing his job.

"I'm going to tell him tonight and if I need you or Tristian, I'll let you know but for right now, just don't say anything to Tristian or my dad," I pleaded with her, because Tristian would body him whether he touched me or not.

"I'm telling you now, Jess, that you have until the end of the week to break things off with him, or I will be telling Tristian what's been going on," she warned and I knew she wasn't playing.

I don't even know why we met up at the bar, because neither one of us had a drink; we were just there to talk. I needed a drink, but I wasn't going to make the mistake of drinking and driving; I just wanted to go to a semi-dark place to vent to my best friend. Once I was back in the car, I felt like I was being followed again, but when I looked through my rearview window, I didn't see anyone following me. I did see a car but it turned off near the corner store, so I tried to calm myself down, knowing that I had to do this because I wasn't about to live like this. I thought about inviting Kylief over to the house to tell him that I didn't think that we could see each other anymore, but I felt it would be safer to just tell him via text. I always said that a female or male should never break up over voicemail, phone, or text, but considering the situation; I feel this would be my best option. I went over in my head what I was going to say in the text and when I finally settled on what I was going to say, I grabbed my phone and decided to send it now before I lost the nerve.

Me- Hey, Kylief wyd?

Damn, I was chickening out already, asking him what he was doing when I wasn't supposed to care what he was doing. I just needed to tell him that it was over and get it over with because I was losing the nerves to tell him.

Kylief- Fuck what I'm doing why the fuck haven't you been answering my calls?

Me- My phone died.

Kylief- Bullshit, if the shit was dead it wouldn't have rung all those fucking times before going to voicemail.

I knew that it was now or never, and being that he was doing the same shit that I despise, it put the battery in my back that I needed to end it with him.

Me- Look Kylief, I can't do this with you anymore and I think it's best that we end our relationship now.

Kylief- What the fuck you mean end our relationship? Are you fucking someone else? I knew it, you fucking with someone at your fucking job, right?

Ugh, I felt like telling him yes, I'm fucking with someone at my job so he'd leave me the fuck alone but being that I had feelings for him, I didn't want to be mean about it.

Me- Kylief, it has nothing to do with me seeing anyone else, it's you. I don't like how you went from being the man that I've grown to love, to the man that is possessive and controlling and I just can't do it anymore. So, please don't call me or text me, I'm done.

Kylief- Can I just come over and we talk about it? Please, Jess.

Me- No Kylief, there is nothing else to talk about, I'm done.

Kylief- So, you really going to let a nigga at your job take you from me, after telling me that you love me, Jess? Don't do this, I'm sorry and I promise that I will stop being so controlling. I just never loved anyone how I love you and I just didn't know how to act, but I promise I'll change my ways. This being in love and being jealous is new to me and it got the best of me, but I promise if you give me another chance, it will not happen again.

I knew that I should have just ended the conversation and stopped responding after I told him we're done, because he had me considering giving him another chance. But if I didn't end it, *Trish was going to tell Tristian what's been going on, so maybe I could just tell her that I ended it with him,* I thought.

Me- Kylief, I swear if you go back to treating me like I'm your property again, I'm done and nothing you can say will change my mind.

Kylief- I promise, Jess. I will treat you the way you deserve to be treated. I'm on my way over.

Me- Ok.

Kylief went back to being the man I fell in love with for a good two weeks, before going back to thinking he owned me. I was now locked in Red Lobster's bathroom, waiting for Trish to get here because this nigga done lost his mind, putting his hands on me. The manager, Jason, just so happened to be someone that I went to high school with and the only thing he said to me was hello and asked how my father was doing. Kylief, in his mind, felt that I disrespected him by flirting in his face like he wasn't sitting there, so when he started threatening Jason, all I said to him was for him to calm down. He took that as me defending Jason and slapped me in front of everyone who was watching him act a fool. Jason threatened to call the cops if he didn't leave, so he barked at me to leave with him but I told him that I wasn't leaving, so he knocked everything off the table before storming out of the restaurant.

My phone alerted me that I had a text message and I thought it was going to be him, but it was Trish, telling me that she just pulled up and that she didn't see his car. I was kind of embarrassed to leave the bathroom because my eye had already started swelling from where he hit me. When I walked out of the bathroom, Jason asked if I was ok and I told him that I was and my whole facial expression changed when I saw that Trish wasn't alone. She'd called Tristian and he was with his friends,

117

Rome and Ramel, so I was kind of relieved that Kylief left, because I didn't want to see Tristian locked up behind my being stupid. I was kind of upset that she called him, but I understood the position that I put her in, so I had no right being upset with her. Tristian looked at me with a pissed-off look on his face as he examined my face.

"Where the fuck that nigga live?" he barked at me, once we were outside of the restaurant.

"Trish, can you please just take me home?" I said, ignoring him and sending him in a rage, and had her looking at me like I had done lost my mind.

"So, you good with that nigga putting his fucking hands on you? Jess, I swear if you don't give me his address right now, I'm calling your father and you already know that's not what you want," he said, knowing that I didn't want my dad involved, because he would have me go to the police station to file charges, so that when he takes Kylief's life it will be justified.

After giving him Kylief's address, he left and I dreaded getting into the car with Trish, because I told her that I ended things with him. She didn't say anything yet, but I could tell she was trying to choose her words, because she was pissed right now.

"Jess, I thought you told me that you left him alone?" she questioned.

"I'm sorry that I lied to you, but he apologized and I just figured that I would give him another chance," I said, sounding like those females that always make excuses for their abusive boyfriends.

"All you did was give him a chance to upgrade from controlling you to putting his fucking hands on you. I just don't understand what the hell is wrong with you, allowing a fucking man to put his hands on you. Was this even the first time that he put his hands on you, Jess?" she asked and I put my head down.

"I can't believe this shit," she yelled, banging her hand on the steering wheel, causing me to jump.

I knew why she was so upset; we used to talk about domestic violence all the time after one of our classmates lost her life to it. We always said that we would never allow a man to put his hand on us, let alone stay with him. She was now giving me the silent treatment as I allowed the tears to leave my eyes, because I was hurt that everyone was mad at me. I was also hurt that Kylief would do me like that when he promised that he would change. I closed my eyes and didn't open them until she pulled up to my house and when I got out of the car, she didn't say anything so I didn't say anything either.

Chapter Fifteen
Demayo

"Why am I here, Kylief? The last time I spoke to you, it was, 'you have a girl and for me to get off your line'," I snapped at his ass, because I was so fed up with him playing with my feelings.

If she left him, it's probably because she found out about his fucking hand problem, but he knew that I didn't put up with him putting his hands on me. I love him to death, but the first time he put his hands on me, I tried to take his fucking head off so he knew if he raised his hands to me, he was in for the fight of his life. I think the reason he broke up with me had nothing to do with me being clingy, because his ass was just as clingy as I was. I think it had to do with him knowing he couldn't control me the way he was used to controlling women. I'm not going to lie and say that he wasn't a good man, because he had the potential to be one, but those bipolar impulses that he has gets in the way of letting him be great. I tried to convince him that nothing was wrong with talking to someone, or even getting medication to help him deal with the impulses, because sometimes it just came out of nowhere.

"Demayo, miss me with the bullshit, acting like you're not happy to be here with a nigga," he barked, causing me to smile because he knew that my pussy got wet just from the sound of his voice so yeah, a bitch was happy. But, it didn't stop me from being pissed about him playing me for the next bitch.

"I'm just saying that you didn't have to play me for another bitch. Even if you weren't feeling me in that moment, you shouldn't have allowed her to do that shit to me."

"So, you must have amnesia because the way I remember it, you attacked her first when she didn't do shit to you, because I had already told you we were done."

"Just to call me back," I mumbled under my breath. "So, are you going to tell me what happened to you?" I asked him, because he was beaten up and they did a job on his face.

"I got robbed leaving the bowling alley the other night," he said, but I didn't believe him because he stayed strapped.

I never mentioned to Toni that her man's best friend, Jess, was now dating my ex, because I was going to use it to my advantage. Being that he's not telling me the truth about what happened to him, I figure I will start up a conversation with

Toni about Jess, since she was always our topic of conversation. I needed to know if Toni knew anything from Tristian about what happened that would tell me what was going on. I needed to know if they broke up, but knowing Tristian, he probably didn't tell her anything even if he knew.

"I need a favor," he said.

"And what's in it for me?" I said, giving him the side eye.

"I don't want my mom seeing me like this because she's going to worry, so I need for you to take her to her doctor appointment tomorrow."

"Fuck no! You know just as well as I do that your mother doesn't like me and I'm sure if I show up to her door, she's going to slam the door in my face," I reminded him.

"I already spoke to her, so she knows that you will be picking her up in the morning."

"So, I'm supposed to just call off work? I'm not about to lose my job by calling off without making a request in the system," I told him. I didn't give a shit about losing my job for him, but he didn't need to know that.

"I got you, just do this shit for me," he barked, letting out an exasperated breath like he was getting pissed, like he wasn't asking me for a favor.

"What else do you have for me?" I said, licking my lips and letting him know that if he wanted me to take his mother to the doctor, he was going to have to come up off that dick.

His face was fucked up but he was still sexy as fuck to me, and his getting his ass kicked wasn't going to deter me from getting mine.

"I'm going to need you to get up out of my personal space," he said, but I ignored him as I released his dick from his sweats and took him into my mouth.

I missed sucking his dick and from the sound of his moans, he missed it too so he could play like he didn't want it, but I knew he did. I played with his balls as I continued to suck the skin off of his shit and he grabbed the back of my head, pumping forcefully into my mouth until he released. After sucking him dry, I removed the pants I was wearing followed by my panties, lowering myself onto his dick and rode him as if it was going to be my last ride. *If this was indeed my last ride, this was going to be a ride he wouldn't forget and I'll bet money on that shit*, I thought as I went back to working his ass.

He groaned as he tried to work his hips, because he was in pain from the beating he took.

"Just enjoy the ride, Kylief, I got this," I whispered in his ear.

He loved to be in control, so I knew this was killing him not being able to be the aggressor like always. I grabbed his head and pushed his face between my breasts, causing him to pull my shirt over my head and lift my bra up, sucking my breast hungrily. I felt myself on the verge of cumming, but I was trying hard to savor the moment, because I didn't know if he was going to give me the dick again. When he grabbed my hips, I knew he was on the verge of exploding too, because he didn't seem bothered by the pain anymore as he bounced me up and down until we both came. I hopped up off him and collapsed on the couch, putting my feet into his lap and trying to catch my breath.

The next day, I was on my way to work after taking his mother to her appointment and I have to say, it wasn't as bad as I thought it was going to be. I mean she didn't have much conversation for me, but she did speak here and there, making me thankful that the appointment only lasted like twenty minutes once she was called to the back. She was there just for a follow-up visit to see if she was feeling any better after being on the medication that her doctor prescribed her, and after giving her a new prescription we were on our way. Kylief was going to have to let his mom know he got his ass kicked, because I didn't take her to fill her prescription so he was going to have to do it. I agreed to take her to the doctor and that's what I did, so my good deed was done for the day.

"Hey, I thought you weren't coming in today," Toni said to me as soon as I walked in.

"I wasn't going to come in, but I finished what I had to do early so I decided to get my coins, even if it's not for a full day," I told her.

"How are you feeling?" I asked her, because she looked stressed.

"Girl, we can talk about it on break," she said, before getting back to servicing the woman with a pissed look on her face, who was at her window..

I wasn't doing teller services today being I came in late, so I was working with tickets for replacement cards. I didn't mind because it never got too busy working in that department, so most of the times I would be on my phone until it was time for break. Toni's meal break was at noon and mine was at one; I wasn't working teller services, but since it wasn't busy I was going at noon too. Toni's ass didn't want to go out to get something to eat anymore since she got pregnant, so she brings her lunch. Since I wanted to be nosey I was just going to tell her I ate already because I wasn't about to miss out on what had her stressed.

"So, what happened?" I asked as soon as she took her food out of the microwave.

"Damn, thirsty, can I sit down first?" she laughed.

"Girl, don't act like you don't know my ass, nosey," I laughed.

"Anyway, you know I been telling you that Tristian's been on his best behavior since my being pregnant, right? So, the other night he comes home and says that he needed to talk to me, so I sit down hoping it's no bullshit, because I don't need no stress while being pregnant. This nigga goes to tell me that the dude that Jess is seeing hit her and he wanted to know how I felt about him staying with her, just to make sure that her boyfriend didn't show up. I got upset because when the bitch got robbed in front of her house and he wanted to stay with her then too, I told his ass no, so I felt some way when he had the nerves to ask again. I understand that she's his friend and if he felt the need to protect her, why not invite her to our home? I

127

would respect that more, but to leave our home to stay with her? Hell no. Do you think that I was wrong?"

I really wasn't listening to nothing she said after Jess' boyfriend hit her, so now I know who beat his ass. I knew his ass only called me because that bitch wasn't fucking with him anymore. He makes me sick and I swear if I didn't love him, I would walk away from his ass for using my ass today. I really didn't want to converse with her any longer because I was now pissed, but I knew if I didn't say something, she was going to know something was up.

"Toni, I don't think that you're wrong, but you do have to understand that Jess is his best friend and he's probably always been her protector. I understand your position, but you don't need to put him in a position where he feels like he should choose, because I promise you he will choose her and you don't want that. What you should have done was been the one that extended the invitation for her to stay with you guys. Even if you didn't mean it, the gesture alone would have shown him that you cared about the safety of his friend's wellbeing the same as he did. So, what he's probably doing now is despising you because he couldn't be there for his friend the way that he's used to being there for her. She probably would have declined the invitation, so yeah, that's the route I would have taken. Also, that would have shown him that you trust him again and shit would have been good," I advised her, because she didn't know how to play the game.

"I get what you are saying, but I wasn't thinking like that. I do understand that she's his friend and she was here before me but when he asked, it just felt like a slap in the face. I just feel like at some point in our relationship, he should consider my feelings before hers and especially now that we're about to have a baby. So, if we decide to get married, does that mean that I'm still going to have to come second in his life? It's just not fair and that's all I be trying to get him to understand, but when it comes to her; my opinion just don't matter. He will hear it but he doesn't respect it, instead he gets upset with me for having the wrong opinion, in his eyes," she said, letting a few tears fall.

"Don't cry, Toni, you just have to start expressing your feelings to him the same way that you express them to me. Men are slow and he may be loyal to his best friend, but he has a responsibility not to make you feel that she comes before you. I promise you, the next time that he says that he's going to check on her or going to kick it with her, say some shit like why don't you invite her over here? Be like, I'll cook something and we could watch a movie or play some cards or something. You could go as far as saying, it's about time I get to know her if she's going to be our baby's godmother, because you know that nigga is going to be making her the godmother," I said, causing a frown on her face. "Trust me, baby girl; that shit will work, I'll put money on it," I told her, but it was up to her to use what I was telling her.

After break was over, I wanted to hit Kylief up and tell his ass that I didn't appreciate him using me, because the bitch broke up with him. But after thinking about it I decided not to, because even if she didn't break up with him, if he called I would have went running anyway. Now that she broke up with him, maybe I could get him to see that he made a mistake by breaking up with me. I know I was acting desperate, but my feelings for him never changed and I never really understand why he broke up with me over something that I could have fixed. If I could put up with his bipolar behavior, he could have put up with me having a problem with him never being home. It wasn't even like I was nagging him every day; it was just once in a while, especially when he would make plans with me and never show up, or have me cook dinner and then I don't see him until the next night. I only had a few hours left at work, so I decided not to sit there and dwell on Kylief's ass as I took the next ticket.

Chapter Sixteen
Kylief

"Good morning, you've reached B & B law firm. How may I direct your call?" Jess sang through the phone.

"Good morning, Jess. I'm sorry to be calling you at work, but you gave me no other choice. I just wanted to call and apologize to you. I should have never put my hands on you," I finally spoke into the phone.

"Kylief, I'm at work and I can't do this with you right now," she said, ending the call and pissing me off.

I wanted to call her back but I knew if I called, she would say that I was being aggressive again. I just decided to send her some flowers with a card, asking her to call me when she was ready to talk to me. I was pissed that she sent her goons to see me but it's all good, because I will deal with that accordingly, but for right now I just needed my girl back. Those dudes only caught me slipping because I had ordered take-out so I thought that's who was knocking at my front door, but it was those fuck niggas. Dude wanted me to know it was him, because he didn't even wear anything to cover his face and that was his first mistake. His second mistake was leaving me breathing, and his third was fucking with a nigga like me, because I'm going to hit him back where the shit hurts. Now that my face was looking better, I was on my way to my mom's crib so I could see how she's doing and pick up the prescription that dumb ass Demayo didn't take her to get filled. Demayo's been ringing my phone again, but I've just been ignoring her calls because she served her purpose and even got some dick for her services, so she should be good. I don't know what made her think that I wanted to get back with her; just because I called her for a favor that she half-ass did anyway. I should have known her delusional ass would make it more than what it was, especially since I slipped up and gave her the dick.

My mom answered the door, wearing a scarf wrapped around her head, with a robe and slippers in the middle of the day. I knew that meant that she wasn't feeling well, pissing me off that Demayo didn't get the new prescription filled.

"Hey Mom," I greeted her with a kiss on her cheek.

"How are you doing, son?" she asked me, but I was more concerned about how she was doing.

"Mom, I'm feeling better now, but how are you doing?" I answered remembering that I told her I wasn't feeling well and that's why I couldn't take her to the doctor.

"I'm feeling somewhat better and my appetite has gotten better, but I just can't shake this nausea feeling. I'm thinking that maybe I should get a second opinion, because the first medication didn't work and I promise you that the other one will have the same results," she stressed.

"Well Mom, make an appointment at New York Presbyterian like I suggested before you started going to that hole-in-the-wall doctor's office," I told her.

"I just didn't want to put you out of your way, because that hospital is pretty far," she said.

"Mom, you don't have to worry about how far it is, just make the appointment so that we could see what's really going on with you."

"So, why did you get Demayo to take me to the doctor, and what happened to the Jess girl that you told me you started seeing?" she asked me.

"Jess left me, and Demayo's crazy behind was the only other person I trusted to take you to the doctor," I answered.

"Left you? Ky baby, your eyes lit up when you spoke of that girl, so what did you do?" she asked, but I'm sure she already knew.

"I let my anger get the best of me and I hit her, but I promise you that I didn't mean it, Mom. I tried to apologize to her, but she's not speaking to me and refuses to see me," I said, telling her the truth.

"Ky! Are you taking your medication, baby, because you know when you don't take your medication you have no control over your emotions? I need for you to take care of yourself, Ky, because you can't afford to get into any more trouble, son," she said, with disappointment in her voice.

"Mom, I can't run a business with the way those pills be making me feel and you know that," I said, not wanting to talk about it.

"Baby, all I want is what's best for you just like you want nothing but the same for me, so if those pills are too strong, maybe you should go back to the doctor," she suggested, but I was done with those pills because I had this shit under control.

After leaving my mother's house, it was time for me to go and handle my business, so this fuck nigga can feel my wrath. He must have thought I was some punk nigga, but I'm about to show him that I don't need an army to handle my shit like his ass needed. I pulled up to the address that my dude, Rah, gave me and now I was sitting outside, until it was time for me to handle the shit. I couldn't believe that I sat in the car for two hours until night fell, but I needed to make sure that no one left or came into the home. My homeboy already confirmed that dude's mom was home, so once I saw the bedroom light go out it was on and popping. I'm about to hit that nigga where it hurts to teach that nigga what happens between me and my bitch isn't his business. I got out of the car and crept towards the back of the house and popped the door without any issues. The back door led me through the kitchen where I stood to pull out my gun, attaching the silencer before going towards the bedroom.

I stood outside of the bedroom and I noticed from the light coming from the television that she wasn't in bed alone. A man was sleeping soundly next to her with his arm wrapped around her in a spooning position, but I didn't give a fuck. Whoever the hell he was, he just happened to be in the wrong place at the wrong time and I didn't have time to worry about it, because I'd been in the house longer than I expected to be already. I walked over to the bed, putting a bullet in both their heads before getting the fuck up out of there, making sure not to be seen going out the back door.

Once I made it home, I removed the gloves that I was wearing and threw them in the trash and removed the watch and a wallet that I took off the dresser at the home. I wrapped both the watch and the wallet into a towel and hid it in the back of my linen closet. I didn't care if they ruled it a robbery or not, I just wanted a souvenir just in case I felt the need to taunt that nigga about murdering his fucking mother and whoever dude was that she was smashing. After I got out of the shower, I went downstairs to pour me a shot of Hennessy and roll a blunt before going back upstairs to chill. I tried calling Jess, but she sent my call straight to voicemail pissing me off, because I didn't understand why the fuck she couldn't just get over the shit. I was going to give her one more chance to answer the phone tomorrow and speak to me and if she refused, I was just going to show up to her job. My phone rang and it was crazy ass Demayo so I ignored her call, putting my phone down, but it just stopped and rang again.

"What!" I screamed into the phone.

"Damn, it's like that after I did your ass a fucking favor," she whined.

"Demayo, either you tell me what the fuck you want or get off my line," I shouted.

"I just wanted to know if you were up for some company," she said and although I didn't want to fuck with her on that level again, I told her to come through.

I knew that I was careful with how I just handled my business, but sometimes you can never be too careful. If anything happened to come back to me about tonight, this bitch would be my alibi, but I doubt that it's going to come to that. The only problem with letting her come through is she'd be thinking that I wanted to get with her again and that wasn't the case.

Chapter Seventeen
Jess

I didn't even get the sleep out of my eyes before my phone starting ringing, causing me to let go of an exasperated sigh, hoping it wasn't Kylief. I didn't want to talk to him and was relieved to see that it was Trish calling and not his ass.

"Hey," I paused, hearing her sniffling into the phone as if she's been crying.

"Trish, what's wrong?" I asked, getting worried as tears filled my eyes because if Trish was crying, I knew that it had to be serious.

She attempted to tell me what was wrong, but she broke down and the next thing I heard was Toni on the phone, telling me to get to Mama Bear's house. When I arrived at Mama Bear's house, my heart fell into my stomach upon seeing police and the ambulance out front. I attempted to go into the house, but the officer wasn't allowing anyone in until I heard Tristian's bark, telling him to let me through.

"What happened?" I cried, knowing that it wasn't good.

"I came home this morning and noticed that Mom's car was still here, but when I came inside and called out to her, she didn't answer. I figured that her and your dad was still sleeping, because his car was here as well. Something just kept telling me to check on them, so I went upstairs and found them both in bed dead," Trish explained, causing the room to start spinning as the tears rushed from my eyes.

I ran up the stairs so fast, only to be stopped by Tristian, but I started fighting him because I needed to see my father.

"Jess, you don't need to see them like that," he said as he held onto me, not trying to let me go.

"Tristian, let me go; my father needs me," I cried uncontrollably. "Daddy," I yelled as I got out of Tristian's arms and ran to the room.

When I walked into the room and saw my dad and Mama Bear, I lost it because I just couldn't believe that someone would do this to them. They wouldn't hurt anyone and it hurt me to my core so much that my chest started to feel tight and I felt like I couldn't breathe. I collapsed in the middle of the floor, crying my heart out because the pain was too much to bear. Tristian got down on the floor and cradled me into his arms letting me get it all out, until the officer told him that we couldn't be in the room because this was a crime scene. I could tell he was trying to be sympathetic, but he had a job to do and if I wanted whoever done this to be caught, I needed to respect it. Tristian, Trish, Toni, and I were now sitting in the living room on numb as we tried to come to grips that they were gone, but didn't know how. I cried so much that my eyes were now burning and I just wanted to go home, because Tristian had Toni and Mekhi just arrived to be with Trish. I wanted to crawl into my bed and pull the covers over my head and stop breathing to go and be with my Mom, Dad and Mama Bear because this was so hard. I felt like I had no one left, so what purpose did I have left on this green earth, when I have nothing or no one to live for right now.

The officers said that it was a home invasion, making me wonder if it was a targeted hit because they never stayed at Mama Bear's house together. I didn't even go home; I decided to go to my dad's house and as I sat outside his house, the tears just fell from my eyes. *What was I going to do with my father not being here anymore?* I knew I needed to be strong because that's what he would have wanted, but how do you be strong after losing someone that meant the world to you? After finding the strength to get out of the car, I dug into my purse for the keys to go inside, but stopped when my phone alerted me that I had a text message.

Tristian- I'm at your crib. Wya?

Me- I'm sitting in my car outside my dad's house about to go inside.

Tristian- I'm on my way.

As soon as I walked through the front door, the smell of his Fahrenheit Cologne sent me into an emotional outburst as I cried out for my daddy. This shit was unreal and so fucking unfair as anger began to sink in and in this very moment, I felt like murdering someone. If I knew who was responsible, I swear I would take their life without a second thought. They could have taken whatever they wanted, without killing two people who would have given them the shirts off their back, with no questions asked. Sitting on the sofa, my eyes focused on the wedding magazine that was sitting on the table and I felt so bad that Mama Bear didn't get to get her dream of walking down the aisle. She was so excited about being my father's wife and this shit just hurt that someone took her dream away for their selfish reasons. I tried not to cry anymore, but the tears just wouldn't stop as I cried for them both, because they would never get to live out that dream of being husband and wife. She was also excited about being a grandmother and now she's not here to see her first grandchild born, because of some fucking loser.

Tristian texted me to open the door so I got up to let him in and he looked a mess. I knew he was trying to be strong for Trish and me, but his eyes were now bloodshot red, letting me know that he had his moment too. He looked at me with sad eyes that matched mine, pulling me into him as we both stood there feeling each other's pain.

"This shit is so not fair," I shouted, pulling myself out of his arms.

I didn't want to be comforted; I wanted someone to pay and I wanted him to know how angry I was. No, it wasn't his fault but I wanted to hear from his mouth that whoever did this was going to pay with their life. He knew me and he knew what I needed, because those were the words that came out of his mouth, giving me some relief that someone would pay. Even if he never found out who did it, it was something that I needed to hear, because I knew that if he found that person, they would be dealt with.

"Trish wants us to get together tomorrow so that we could make the arrangements," he said, but I didn't want to talk about that, because I haven't come to grips that they were gone.

"I know that this is our reality right now, but I just don't want to talk about this right now," I told him, because that's how I was feeling.

"We don't have to talk about it right now, but it's something that's going to have to be done," he said, wiping the tears that fell from my eyes.

He went from wiping my tears to kissing them away and when I felt his lips on mine, I didn't stop him. I don't know if it was because of my needing to feel like I wasn't alone that I didn't stop him, but it was what I needed right now. When he slipped his tongue into my mouth, I returned the kiss as the tears continued to fall from my eyes. I knew what we were doing was wrong but I needed him right now, so I ignored all thoughts of what I was about to do. He undressed me slowly as he laid me down on the couch, and I couldn't stop the tears as he slid inside of me slowly. He continued to kiss my tears away, not missing a beat as he pumped in and out of me. I wrapped my legs behind his back as I gyrated my hips into him, enjoying how he was making me feel and I didn't want it to end.

"I love you," he panted in my ear but I chalked it up to him being caught up in the moment as I closed my eyes, enjoying how my body was feeling right now.

The next morning, we were both still on the couch with him still inside of me; I don't know how that happened. As soon as I moved, I felt his dick growing inside of me and after realizing that last night was a mistake, all I wanted to do was get up from under him. I tapped him on his shoulder and called his name, but instead of him getting up, he started working his dick inside of me.

"Tristian, you need to…oh my God, Tristian…you need to stop," I moaned, trying hard not to give in to how he had me feeling again, as guilt started to seep in.

I'm not lying; I really tried hard to stop it from happening again, but it felt so good that I couldn't resist as I found myself wrapping my legs around his back again. He kissed me deeply, fucking me until his dick went limp inside of me again, and I wasted no time getting up and making my way to the bathroom. I apologized to my dad in my head, because the shit was just wrong to be fucking in his home when he'd just lost his life. I just couldn't believe that we allowed ourselves to cross that line, knowing that it could possibly ruin our friendship. After I showered, I went into the room I kept here

~~here~~ and changed my clothes, trying not to dwell on having to make his funeral arrangements today. Tristian peeked his head into the bedroom to ask if I was ok, before telling me he was going home to shower and change. He added that he would see me later at Mama Bear's house, so I just told him that I was ok, but I wasn't ok and I wouldn't be ok for a very long time.

My phone rang and I saw that it was Kylief calling and even though I didn't want to speak to him, I answered the call anyway.

"Hello," I answered.

"Hey, Jess; I been trying to reach you to see if we were good. I really feel bad how shit between us went down," he said, like I played a part in why we weren't together anymore.

"Kylief, I really don't have time to talk about that now because I'm dealing with something," I told him as a few tears fell.

"Are you ok?" he asked, because I was now on the phone, letting my emotions get the best of me.

"No, I'm not ok; my father was killed last night and so was Tristian and Trish's mom," I sobbed as my lips trembled.

"I'm so sorry for your loss, Jess. I know that we are not on the best of terms right now, but let me come be there for you," he begged.

"I have to meet up with Trish to make funeral arrangements, but you could meet me at my house later," I told him.

I didn't want to be alone and after what happened between Tristian and me, I wouldn't dare ask him to come stay with me. I went into my dad's room to get his important papers that he kept in a manila folder up in the top of his closet. He always told me where to find everything that I would need if something happened to him, but I never imagined that I would be needing those papers so soon.

When I got to Mama Bear's house Tristian and Trish were ~~where~~ already there and she looked just as bad as I did. I really didn't know how any of us was going to get through not having our parents in our lives anymore.

"How are you feeling?" I asked, hugging her and not wanting to let go.

"I'm not doing good, but I know I have to be strong, so that we could handle everything that needs to be handled," she responded.

"Same here, but I say that we just get through this together, because I know I can't do this without the two of you." I couldn't make eye contact with Tristian because I felt guilty about the vulnerable moment that we'd both shared. See, this is the reason I never wanted to take it there with him.

Chapter Eighteen
Tristian

I parked my car behind the limo after returning from the burial, waiting for my sister so that I could drop her off at the house to get things ready for the repast. I refused to ride in the limo because I couldn't believe that Jess had this nigga with her, allowing his punk ass to comfort her. I swear if it wasn't my mom and her dad's funerals, I would have ended that nigga because I let him know to stay the fuck away from her. I also told his ass that if I saw him anywhere near her again, he wasn't going to be so lucky next time but here this bold motherfucker was, not taking heed to my warning. I just felt disrespected by them both, but mostly her ass because after dude put hands on her, she had the nerve to have him here and not to mention, the fact that we shared a night together. I was just so confused as to why she would run back to him like she needed him when she didn't. If she needed someone to lean on, Trish and I were here for her so his services weren't needed, unless this was her way of avoiding what happened between us.

Toni was upset with me about not coming home that night, but she was here to support me today but I didn't want or need it. I was too focused on what Jess had going on and I knew I needed to get my shit together, knowing that I was about to be a father. If I lost Toni, I knew that she was going to give me a tough time when it came to being in my son's life, so I needed to make this shit right with her, as soon as I got at Jess to find out what the fuck was going on with her and this decision that she made. After Trish got into the car, I pulled out to take her to the house so that she could help Mekhi set up before people started to get there. I told her that I would be back in a few because Toni wasn't feeling well, so she was going to go home to lay down, but I knew Toni was fine; she just wanted to go home.

"So, what's going on with you and Jess?" Toni asked, once we got to the house.

"What do you mean, what's going on with me and Jess?" I asked, annoyed.

I knew she was referring to Jess and me not speaking or giving eye contact, being that we claim to be best friends. I wasn't feeling Jess right now and anyone watching both of us like Toni seemed to have been doing would have picked up on it too.

149

"You didn't even speak to her and she didn't speak to you, so I just find it strange that at this delicate time that you two wouldn't be speaking. So, again, what's going on with you and Jess?" she said, not letting it go even after hearing the annoyance in my voice.

"Toni, nothing is going on between us; we both are dealing with the loss of our parents and that's it," I lied.

"Yeah ok," she said with a roll of her eyes, wobbling away.

I really didn't want to go back to the house, but I knew that no matter how I felt at this point, I needed to be there for my sister. I called out to let Toni know that I was leaving but she didn't respond. So, I just left, not wanting to get into an argument, stressing her out any more than I already had.

I walked into my mom's house and there were quite a few people from their jobs that came back to the house. Trish and Jess were in the kitchen fixing plates and I was glad to see that she had sense enough not to bring that nigga here. Our eyes met briefly, but she turned her head to avoid any further eye contact as she waked out of the kitchen, so I decided to just check on my sister to make sure she was good.

"You good, sis?" I asked her.

"Bro, I don't think I'm ever going to be good as long as I have to come home and not see Mom here. I sat at the funeral and attended the burial, but I still can't come to grips that she's really gone. I just keep thinking of all the what-ifs because had I been here, maybe it wouldn't have happened."

"Trish, don't do that because it sounds like you're blaming yourself; you had no way of knowing that the shit was going to happen, so you don't know that your being here would've made a difference. Had you been here, I would probably have been burying you too. I still can't believe that she's gone, same as you, but we have to keep living just as she would want us to do," I let her know, trying not to get too emotional.

"I'm trying," was all she said as she went back to what she was doing.

I needed a damn blunt because the way I was feeling about my mom, and the way I wanted to feel my dick inside of Jess again had me tripping. I tried not to think about what happened between Jess and me, but it was hard and it was bothering me that she was still walking around avoiding me.

After everyone left and Trish wasn't around, I cornered her ass in the kitchen because she was going to stop acting like she had an issue with me.

"So, why do you have that nigga in your space again?" I asked her, when I really wanted to ask her how she was feeling first, but fuck that.

"Tristian, now is not the time," she said, trying to walk around me but I stopped her.

"So, is it the right time to tell me why you're avoiding me? Are you tripping about what happened between us?" I asked, waiting for her to tell me something.

"It shouldn't have happened, Tristian."

"And why not?"

"For starters, you have a girlfriend with a child on the way and second, we're family," she said, pissing me off.

"We are not fucking family, so I wished that you would stop saying that shit. We are friends and had you not kept putting me in the family bracket, and acted on the feelings that we have for each other, there would be no girl and baby on the way," I snapped.

Whenever she didn't want to deal with the feelings that she knows that she has for me, she starts kicking that family shit. Yes, I consider her close enough to be family, but at the end of the fucking day, we are not blood-related. I didn't mean to snap like that, but I was getting tired of her continuing to front on me.

"Whether we are family or not, it doesn't change the fact that you have a girl and I have a man," she snapped back.

"Oh, so now you have a man? Because last I checked, you had a fuck boy that put his hands on you, so I hope you didn't take him back." I looked at her like she done lost her mind.

"He apologized," she had the nerve to say.

"They always apologize, but that's doesn't mean that he's not going to do it again. Why the fuck would you have me put hands on him, just for you to take his ass back?" I yelled at her.

"I didn't tell you to put hands on him; you did that all on your own calling yourself protecting me, so that was your decision. I didn't even call you to the restaurant that day, so how could you say that I had you put hands on him?"

"You didn't have to tell me to put hands on him, but you knew what was going to happen if you said that he hit you. Your father would be so disappointed in you right now, because he didn't raise you to be this fucking stupid," I said and regretted it as soon as the words left my mouth.

I let my anger get the best of me and the hurt displayed on her face made me feel like shit as the tears fell from her eyes. She was in fact being stupid, but now wasn't the time to say the shit and tell her that her father, who just passed away would be disappointed in her, so I needed to apologize.

"I'm sorry, Jess, I didn't mean to make you cry. I just feel that you shouldn't be giving that nigga a second chance to do the same shit to you again," I said to her.

I knew that I shouldn't have thought about pulling her into me, because it was going to be hard not kiss her tears away again, but I needed to comfort her. As soon as I pulled her into me and she didn't hesitate to be in my arms, I kissed the nape of her neck before finding her lips as we stood in the kitchen kissing.

"Um...um..." we heard my sister clearing her throat. "What's going on here?" she asked, with a mischievous smirk on her face.

"Nothing is going on," Jess answered, moving away from me.

"Well, it didn't look like nothing to me, because it looked like Tristian was trying to swallow your face whole," she said, laughing at her own joke.

"We were just talking, Trish," I said to her.

"Ok, if you say so, but all I'm going to say is that I wouldn't want it any other way. Jess is already my sister, so to add in-law to it works for me," she said in a matter-of-fact tone.

"Trish, your brother is already spoken for with a child on the way, and Kylief and I are trying to work on staying together," Jess said.

"Jess, I don't need a recap on what I already know, because I'm sure that you knew all of that also, before you stood in this kitchen kissing him. So, what's really going on?" she directed her question to Jess and I wanted to know too.

"I don't know," Jess answered, grabbing her bag and leaving out the front door

Chapter Nineteen
Jess

I hated the way I left from Mama Bear's house, but I needed some air and to get out of Trish's line of questioning. Once she started, it was a wrap from there. If anybody knew how I really felt about Tristian, it would be Trish; she never had a problem calling me on it and tonight wouldn't have been any different. I didn't want Tristian to know how I really felt, because it wouldn't be fair to admit those feelings to him now, because all it would do is force his hand and I'm almost certain that he would pick me. It was wrong to let my emotions and feelings for him, put me in the situation that led us to sleeping together the other night.

I decided not to think about it for the rest of the night as I pulled up to the Exxon gas station to get gas before heading to Kylief's place. I called him to let him know that I didn't want to be home alone tonight, so he offered and I accepted. Coming out of the gas station after paying for my gas, I noticed that there was a woman standing near my car and I swear, I wasn't in the mood to hear a "sob, I'm homeless" story. As I neared my car, I noticed that the woman didn't appear to be homeless, because she was dressed nicely and her hair was laid, so it left me wondering what she wanted. I tried to see if I recognized her, but as I got closer I realized that I didn't know her, leaving me to put my guard up, because I didn't need a repeat of what happened to me when Demayo attacked me.

"I'm sorry to bother you, but I just wanted to ask you a question if that's alright?" she said to me.

"And what might the question be?" I asked, giving her the side eye because I didn't know her, so what could she possibly want to ask me?

"I saw you a few months ago at K Lanes bowling alley with Kylief and just wanted to know if you're dating him?" she asked.

"Why would that be any concern of yours?" I asked, becoming very defensive at this point, because I wasn't sure what was to come next. I wasn't about to have another fight with a female who was claiming to be with Kylief again, so if that's what her line of questioning was about, she could keep it moving.

"I'm not here to argue or fight with you about Kylief, but I do think that you need to allow me to speak to you about him.

Kylief isn't the man that he portrays himself to be and as long as I'm breathing, I'm going to make sure that another woman doesn't become a victim like my sister," she said and now I was all ears.

She suggested that I meet her at the diner that was just around the corner, so that she could talk to me. I knew that I shouldn't have agreed being that I didn't know her, but she seemed sincere enough so I followed her to the diner. We were now sitting down and I was waiting for her to tell me what she needed to tell me about Kylief.

"First, let me say that I'm sorry for just invading your space today, but when I saw that Kylief was dating again, I just couldn't sit back and say nothing. My name is Kenya and my sister, Serena, was dating Kylief for four years and in the beginning, the relationship was great because they seemed to be in love. A year into the relationship, Kylief became very abusive and my family and I tried to get Serena to leave, but she just kept insisting that she loved him and that he didn't mean it and promised to never do it again. It got to the point to where my sister had become his personal punching bag and we were finally able to convince her to leave, but he kept harassing her, threatening her and showing up to her job and home. My mother was fed up with how he was treating Serena, so she took my sister down to the courthouse to file an order of protection against him and I think that took him over the top. My sister went missing from work, never making it home and after the police searched for her for about a week, her body was found in a deserted area in Central Park by a jogger," she finished as she wiped at the tears that fell from her eyes.

"No disrespect to your family, but was Kylief charged with her murder?" I needed to know.

"Kylief was questioned in her murder and he claimed that he was out of town at the time, so they had no choice but to let him go, pending an investigation. About a week later, Kylief was arrested and charged with violating the order of protection, based on a video showing him and my sister arguing the day that she was reported missing. My family and I feel in our hearts that he's responsible for her death, but due to lack of evidence, he wasn't charged for her murder and that crushed my family. I've only seen him with one other woman before you and I tried to warn her about what kind of man Kylief is, but she blew me off. I'm not telling you who you can date and can't date, but I feel it's only right to warn you the same as I tried to warn her," she finished, but I still wasn't convinced that he was capable of murder.

"Did you meet his mother yet?" she asked me.

159

"No, I haven't," I responded.

"Well, my sister had the pleasure of meeting his mother, and his own mother told her that her son had issues. She went as far as telling her that her son was on medication, so I just felt that if this man's mother was telling this to my sister, then she should have believed her. My sister was so blinded by love that she didn't see him for who he really was and it cost her, her life. All I'm trying to do is prevent it from happening to another female. I appreciate you hearing me out and I just pray that if you continue to date him, that you'll be careful and if he put his hands on you, please know if it happened once it will happen again," she finished, before getting up and leaving the diner, leaving me to my thoughts.

After listening to her, I had no idea if what this woman was saying was true, but it was enough for me to decide not to go to Kylief's house tonight. I got into my car and drove home with what Kenya told me weighing heavily on my mind. Kylief called my phone but I ignored his call, deciding that it would be best to play it safe for right now, until I could at least investigate some of what I was told tonight. I called Trish up to tell her what I was told and she told me that I needed to take heed to what the female told me and to leave him alone. She already believed that he was off his rocker, after what her boyfriend told her about what he said to him that night at the restaurant, and the bad vibe that she got from him, so it wasn't hard for her to believe that he was capable of what Kenya accused him of. After hanging up with her, I stopped to get something to eat before going home, because I didn't eat at the repast and although I didn't feel like eating, I needed to satisfy my growling stomach. Now that I think of it, I didn't eat anything at all today.

I had a few missed calls from Kylief so after eating; I decided to give him a call back because I knew if I didn't, he would just keep calling.

"Hey, I thought you were coming through," he said, answering the call.

"I'm sorry, I decided to just come home," I told him, not feeling the need to offer any other explanation.

"So, how about I come over to be with you, because I don't think you should be alone after burying your father today," he offered.

"I'm not feeling up to any company tonight, but tomorrow night I might feel a little better," I tried to convince him, hoping he would just get over that I didn't want to see him.

"I'm not just some fucking company, Jess, I'm supposed to be your man," he snapped, sending a chill throughout my body.

I didn't know if I was still on edge from what Kenya told me about him that caused me to feel that frightening chill. But what I did know was that I didn't like the tone he was using and his ass will not be visiting me tonight.

"I'm sorry, I didn't mean to snap at you; it's just that I don't want you alone when you don't have to be," he said, now trying to justify his getting pissed that I didn't want to see him.

"It's ok and I'm not trying to push you away, Kylief. I just need this time alone," I told him, trying not to agitate him any further.

"Fine, Jess, call me if you need me," he said, sounding pissed before ending the call.

Kenya's words echoed in my head as I went to check all the windows, as well as the front and back door. Once I felt that everything was secure, I went upstairs to shower and got into bed because I had to work in the morning. My boss gave me the rest of the week off, but I declined because I needed to stay busy. I had plans of moving into my family home within the next month, because I couldn't bear the thought of selling it. So many memories were made in that home, so it was only right that I stay there and not sell to a stranger.

Waking up the next morning, I put the television on the news as I did every morning before work and this morning was no different. I walked into the bathroom to brush my teeth and wash my face, before heading back into the bedroom to get a bra and a pair of panties. I briefly looked at the television and something caught my eye as I grabbed the remote to turn up the sound because it was low.

A woman was found shot to death inside of her car late Tuesday evening outside of her family home. Officials said the woman, twenty-nine-year-old Kenya Harris was in the driver's seat and was pronounced dead at the scene. Police responded to several 911 calls regarding shots fired into a vehicle. Witnesses reported seeing a black car leaving the scene, but were unable to confirm the make or model of the car.

I was in shock and couldn't move as my eyes stayed glued to the television, so much so that I had to forcefully drag my eyes away from the screen. What were the odds after talking to this woman about Kylief, she ends up dead? Could Kylief be responsible for her murder? Maybe he followed me and saw her talking to me and knew that she was telling me that she believed he killed her sister. I had so many thoughts going through my head and I honestly started to fear for my life as I picked up my phone to call Trish.

After getting off the phone with Trish, she advised me to call my boss and tell him that I decided to take the rest of the week off. She told me to meet her at Mama Bear's house. She convinced me that I needed to speak to the police, being that I was probably the last person to see her alive, other than the person responsible for killing her. I felt so bad for her family as I watched them outside of the home, breaking down. It had to be hard on the parents since they'd already lost a daughter, just to lose another one.

When I opened my front door, I let out a loud scream at the sight of Kylief standing there with a scowl on his face. He scared the shit out of me, because I wasn't expecting him to be standing outside my door and I was wondering why he was wearing a scowl on his face.

"What are you doing here?" I asked nervously. I'm sure all the color disappeared from my face, because that's how shook I was.

"I came to see if you were in fact ok, because you didn't sound good last night," he said, but the way he said it led me to believe that he didn't believe my excuse last night.

"Kylief, I'm fine and on my way to work," I told him, thinking that he'd take the hint and just leave now that he saw with his own eyes that I was ok, but so much for wishful thinking.

"I don't think you should be driving, so why don't you let me drive you to work and pick you up?" he offered.

I got this unsettling feeling in the pit of my stomach, knowing if I declined he was going to be upset the same as he was on the phone last night. I prayed that his ass just took me to work without any extra bullshit, after telling him that he could take me to work. I'm not going to lie and say that I wasn't scared after what happened to Kenya, and the way he was acting just showing up unannounced after my telling him that I would see him if I felt better later today. I wanted to call Trish so bad, but I didn't want him to say something to me about being on the phone, so again I just prayed that he took me straight to work.

Chapter Twenty
Kylief

"Kylief, where are you going?' Jess asked when she noticed that I was going in the opposite direction of her job.

"Chill, I have to make a stop before taking you to work," I told her and she sucked her teeth and folded her arms against her chest, but I didn't give a fuck.

"Kylief, you're going to make me late for work," she whined, but again I didn't give a fuck.

"Didn't you call your job for the rest of the week off?" I asked her and she started to shift in her seat.

"I did, but decided to go in, but how did you know that I called my job?" she inquired.

"That's not important, but what is important is why you been lying to me."

"Lying to you about what?" she snapped, getting angry.

"You lied about going to work when I just showed up at your door, and last night you said that you changed your mind about coming to my crib, because you wanted to be alone," I reminded her.

"None of what I told you was a lie, my boss gave me the rest of the week off, but I called him to tell him that I would be coming in. And as far as last night, I didn't want any company like I told you, because I wanted to be alone. I did just bury my father, in case you forgot," she said, getting very defensive.

"So, your boss is expecting you this morning?" I asked her as I ignored all that other shit she was saying.

"Yes, he's expecting me and you're going to make me late," she lied as I dialed my phone, making sure it sounded throughout the car.

"What's up?" Luke asked, answering the call.

"Bro, did Jess get to work yet?" I questioned him.

"I told you, she's not coming in for the rest of the week," he said and the look on her face was priceless.

"My bad; I forgot, bro. I'll speak to you later," I said, ending the call.

"What's really good, Jess?" I asked as I pulled up to our destination.

"W-w-where are we?' she stuttered.

"I told you I had a stop to make, so get out of the car and stop questioning me," I barked.

She looked like she wanted to protest getting out of the car, but I gave her a look to let her know that I wasn't bullshitting with her. Her phone was going off and I told her not to answer it, but she looked at me like I was crazy, so I grabbed the shit out of her hand. I pushed her towards the front of the house, ignoring her questions about what we were doing here and how long I was going to be. Once inside, I locked the door, making sure to take the key out of the lock, just in case she had any ideas of making a run for it.

"Kylief, are you going to tell me why we're here?" she asked, getting inpatient with me.

"Yep, as soon as you tell me, what's going on with you? All I've been trying to do is make up for putting my hands on you, but you keep pushing me away," I vented, just wanting her to understand that I was sorry for putting my hands on her.

"Kylief, be honest with yourself for a minute and answer this question truthfully. What would you do if you had a sister and her boyfriend was controlling, verbally abusive and put his hands on her? Would you want her to stay?" she asked, giving me something to think about.

"So, are you saying that I was all those things to you, Jess?" I asked and she tilted her head to the side, giving me a "nigga, you can't be serious" look.

"Although you weren't verbally abusive, you have become controlling and I've told you that. Oh, and you already know that I wasn't exaggerating about you putting your hands on me. So, again, answer my question."

"I wouldn't want my sister to stay in that kind of relationship and I do understand how you feel about the way I've been treating you. Also, I would like you to know that there is a reason behind my madness, besides me being crazy about you." I chuckled lightly from nervousness of telling her the truth, because I never shared what I was about to tell her with anyone.

"And what might that be?" she said and I could tell that she was thinking that I was about to spit some bullshit.

"Growing up, I was diagnosed with a personality disorder, but there were no medications approved by the FDA to treat personality disorders. They had medications that help with some disorder symptoms and in my case, I was given mood stabilizers but for the past few months I haven't been taking them. I'm not making excuses for my behavior, but that's the reason for some of my erratic behavior. I don't want you to think that I kidnapped you, because that's not what I set out to do, but I figured this would be the only way to get you to listen to me."

"So, if you didn't kidnap me, I need to call Trish to let her know that I'm ok, because I was on my way to meet her when you showed up at my house. Also, when I finish letting her know that I'm ok, I need to speak to you as well because I need clarification on a few things."

After she got off the phone with her friend, I took a seat next to her to hear what she had on her mind because it sounded serious. I just knew that she wasn't going to believe me when I said that I had a personality disorder, but if she questioned it, I had the proof.

"So, what's up?" I asked her, prepared to give her the proof as soon as she said that she didn't believe me.

"I was approached by a female yesterday as I was leaving the gas station, and she asked me if she could talk to me about you. She suggested that we meet at a diner that was just around the corner, so against my better judgement, I agreed. She said that her name was Kenya and you dated her sister, Serena, for four years before you killed her. I told her that I didn't believe that you were capable of murder, but this morning when I turned the news on, this same woman was found shot to death in her car outside of her family home." She paused, looking at me for my reaction.

"So, you think that I had something to do with her death, because if that's what you're thinking, you could stop thinking it. I haven't seen Kenya or her family since the day that I was told that it wasn't enough evidence to convict me in the death of her sister," I told her, being honest and wondering why Kenya approached her.

"She said that you were abusive to her sister and that when her sister tried to break it off with you, you killed her," she said and again, I was confused to as why Kenya approached her.

"I didn't kill Serena, but I will admit that a few times altercations with her got out of hand, but Serena held her own each time. Most times, she was the aggressor because of my infidelity back then, so all her family saw from our fights were me being the one abusing her," I told her, because it was the truth and that's the reason she never left me, because she knew the truth.

"Kylief, I want to believe you right now, but to be honest with you, I don't know if I should. I have witnessed first-hand

171

of the temper that you have and you putting your hands on me."

"I already explained to you what was going on with me and to be honest, I didn't mean to put my hands on you. I let how I feel for you and my jealousy of you talking to another man get the best of me. I promise you that I didn't hurt Serena, because at the end of the day I loved her and wouldn't hurt her like that, and when I found out what happened to her, it hurt me. It hurt me even more when her family wouldn't allow me to pay my respects at her funeral. The only thing that I'm guilty of is not being able to keep my dick in my pants at the time, but that's it," I said to her, but she didn't get the chance to respond because my mom walked into the living room.

"Hey, Mom, this is Jess; the one I been telling you about and Jess this is my mom, Vera," I introduced the two.

"Ky, you didn't tell me you would be stopping by today. Nice meeting you, young lady, but this old lady is not feeling well today. I just came down to get a cup of tea and take my medication before retiring back to my bed. I hope to see you again when I'm feeling better," Mom said to her.

"Nice meeting you too and I hope that you feel better soon," Jess said to her.

172

"Mom, you go back upstairs and I'll make you some tea and bring your medication upstairs and Jess, I'll be right back and don't try to make a run for it," I joked.

After making my mom's tea and giving her, her medication, I went back downstairs and Jess was still sitting in the same spot that I left her in. I was hoping that meant that she believed me, because I was telling her the truth about what went down with me and Serena. I was with Serena for four years, like her sister said and I was in love with her, but like I tried to explain to her family; we just had one of those relationships that were up and down. She put her hands on me, I put my hands back on her and that's just the way it was, but I didn't love her any less to the point that I would take her life. I'm not saying that I wasn't capable of taking her life, but there was no need to take her life and to this day, I have no idea who did or they would have gotten dealt with. I just hope that Jess believed me and would decide that we could give our relationship another chance and I prayed that what I did, didn't come back to bite me in the ass. I wasn't too worried that it would, because I do my shit alone and I had no plans on snitching on myself. I did feel kind of bad, because I had no idea that it was her father in that bedroom with that fuck nigga's mother because had I'd known, I would have spared him his life. *I just wanted dude to feel the consequences of putting his fucking hands on me, even if he didn't know that it was me who made him motherless,* I thought as I decided to get back to the matter at hand.

"I don't know if you believe anything that I said to you but just think about this for a second. You thought that I kidnapped you to 'cause you harm, because of what Kenya had you believing about me, right? But as you can see, if I had any intentions of causing you harm, I wouldn't have taken you to my mother's home. I brought you here because had you not believed me when I told you about my condition, I was going to have her tell you that I was telling the truth. She's the reason that I started to take my medication again, because once I told her why we weren't together, she was upset with me and told me that I was going to lose you for good if I didn't get back on my medication. So, now that you know all of this, do you think that we could give this relationship another chance," I pleaded with her.

"Kylief, my only concern at this point is what if you decide that you don't want to be on the medication anymore? I'm not trying to be your personal punching bag, or that person that you continue to treat like your property," she stressed.

"I already told you that I started taking the mood stabilizers again, so you don't have to worry about me treating you the way I've been treating you. I honestly feel like a sucker for putting my hands on you and I'm willing to do everything in my power to prevent it from happening again. That's why I will be taking the medication faithfully," I told her.

"I swear I want to believe you right now because like I told you, I do care for you but I'm scared to do this with you again. I just lost my father to a violent crime and it bothers me that my father died thinking that I was with a man capable of what happened to me the night I was attacked. I defended you, just for you to later put your hands on me, so I'm going to need you to prove my dad wrong because I will not have him turning in his grave, knowing that he was right about you and my still being with you," she told me and I couldn't believe that her peoples would think that I was responsible for her being attacked.

"I promise you that your father will not be turning over in his grave, because like I said earlier, I'm going to do everything in my power to prove it to you. All I need is another chance to show you that I want to be with you and I promise, I will never put my hands on you again," I told her, kissing her lips.

Chapter Twenty-One
Jess

I walked into Mama Bear's house and a wave of sadness washed over me, knowing that I would never see her again. I tried to make little to no eye contact with Tristian once I noticed him sitting in the living room. Had I known that he was here, I would have come at another time, because I wasn't in the mood to ~~get to~~ argue with him. I wanted to talk to Trish but since he was here, I might as well include him in the conversation.

"Hey Jess," Trish said, but she didn't sound good.

"Hey, Trish, how are you holding up?" I asked her.

"I still don't believe that they're gone," she said as her tears fell, causing my tears to fall as well.

"Don't cry, sis, we will get through this together," she said, consoling me when I felt that I should have been consoling her.

It's been a minute since they've been gone but it still felt like it just happened yesterday, every time that I walked into her house. No one knew how hard this was for us to have loving parents, who were always there for us, suddenly gone, and all I wanted to do was wake up from this nightmare we were in. All I have left is Trish and Tristian and I can't stress that enough, but I fear losing them too once they know that Ky and I were back together once again. I know that they don't care for Kylief and don't believe that he deserves another chance, so when I tell them that I decided to forgive him, they may turn their backs on me. I don't know if Trish has been sharing with Tristian about what went down with Kenya and everything else that Kylief confessed to me or not, so I didn't know how he was going to feel.

"Trish, I need to speak with you and Tristian in the living room," I said to her as she followed.

Tristian was already sitting in the living room, doing something on his phone. He looked like he wasn't interested in hearing anything that I had to say, until his sister told him to stop being rude and get off his phone.

"Listen, I just want you guys to know that without a doubt, I will always respect your opinion of anything I have going on in my life. I know that I told you guys before that I decided to give him another chance, but changed my mind about continuing a relationship with him. Trish, you know why I

177

changed my mind, but Kylief and I sat down like I told you and I explained to you what that conversation was about, so we decided to give it another chance. Tristian, I know that this makes you feel some kind of way, being that we slipped up and slept together and trust, I'm not saying that I regret what happened, but I do think that we are better off as just friends."

"Jess, you already know how I feel about him, but if you feel he deserves another chance, then all I could do is respect it. I just pray that you're making the right decision, because I would hate for you to become that girl. You know, the one that makes excuses as to why a man puts his hands on a female, just for it to just keep happening," Trish said.

"I'm not that girl and I will never make excuses for him and if it gets to the point where it happens again, I promise I will walk away. I know that you may not believe me because I lied to you before but after having a conversation as to why it was happening, I feel confident that we are going to be ok," I told her, looking to see if Tristian was going to chime in, but he didn't say anything.

"I'm just going to say this one last thing and then I'm done with it, because I meant it when I said that I was going to respect your decision. I just want to know if you're going to do anything about the female that got murdered after speaking to you? I still feel that you should go to the police and let them know about that conversation that she had with you, on the same day that she lost her life."

"Trish, I had a conversation with Kylief about all of the things that she alleged and he denies doing any of the things she accused him of. He wasn't charged for the murder of her sister, so I think I'm going to just leave it alone," I said to her and I know it sounded like I was making excuses for him but I wasn't, because what I was saying was the truth.

"Tristian, you don't have anything to say?" I asked, getting kind of irritated because he was pissing me off. He had so much to say the other day, but now he just sat there playing on his phone.

"What do you want me to say, Jess, because it's not like we didn't have this conversation before and it changed what? I get it when you say that we are better off as friends and that we shouldn't make a big deal about us fucking each other, because at the end of the day it's that fuck nigga you want to be with. You were right when you said that I have a girl whose about to have my shorty, so I'm not sweating the small shit. So if you say that the nigga is good on not putting his hands on you again, good for you. If you don't believe none of what another female told you, about what was going on with her sister and her being murdered the same night, Jess, I'm cool with that too," he said, getting up all in his feelings and leaving out of the house, leaving me standing there with my mouth open.

I knew that he wasn't going to be happy hearing that I was getting back with Kylief, but I didn't expect him to come at me like that. I didn't want him to think that the night at my father's house didn't mean anything to me, because it did. I just feel that we are better off as friends, because I just couldn't see myself taking him away from Toni, knowing that she was about to have his baby. My feelings were kind of hurt that he ran up out of here, instead of continuing the conversation, *but it is what it is*, I thought, as I focused my attention back to Trish who was waving her hand in front of my face.

"Jess, have you decided when you're moving back into your father's house yet?" she asked and I knew that she was only trying to get me out of my feelings behind how her brother just acted.

"I started packing, so it shouldn't be no later than next weekend, because I still have to sort out his things before moving in. I want to donate his clothes to Goodwill and whatever furniture I decide not to keep, I want to donate it to a few thrift shops," I told her, knowing that it was going to be hard parting with his things.

"Give me a sec," she said, holding her finger up to stop me from saying anything else as she answered her phone.

She left out of the room so I sat on the couch and dialed Tristian's number. I just knew that he wasn't going to answer, so when he did, I was on mute. I was prepared to just leave him a voicemail but now that he answered, I needed to find my voice.

"Are you going to say something or just listen to me breathe?" he barked into the phone.

"I didn't think that you were going to answer," I answered.

"Well, I answered so what's up?" he said, no longer sounding like he was pissed at me.

"I just wanted to call you to tell you that I didn't want you to be mad at me," I told him.

"Jess, I'm not mad at you. I'm just disappointed with you right now, because I didn't expect you to be gullible enough to believe that he would never put hands on you again. If he wasn't capable of it, trust me; it would have never happened, because a real man would have just walked away angry, the same way I just did. I wanted to knock your head off but what did I do, I got my ass up and walked out to calm down and now I'm over it. Nah, but seriously, I just feel that his ass doesn't deserve another chance, but I'm going to be like Trish and respect your decision," he said.

"Friends again?" I asked.

"Friends," he said, causing me to smile.

"Ok, I will talk to you later," I said before ending the call, feeling a whole lot better.

"I'm sorry about that," Trish said, coming back into the room.

"No problem. I used that time to call your brother to smooth things over between us," I said to her.

"I told you how he feels about you; that's why I don't understand why you would take it there with him, knowing he would take it to mean something else. That boy would drop Toni at the drop of a dime, if you mouthed the words that you wanted to see where the relationship could go," she said, sounding like she was pissed with me too.

"Your brother and I both were in a vulnerable state, so I wasn't thinking of the consequences of our actions at the time. We just made up so hopefully, we could go back to just being friends the same as we've always been. Anyway, what are you about to get into, because we haven't hung out since the double-date so we should go shopping or something," I said to her, ready to stop talking about Tristian, before it went to my telling her my true feelings about the situation and how I felt that she was blaming me.

We ended up going to Queens Center Mall to do some shopping and were now headed to Red Lobster to get something to eat. Kylief called and I told him that I was out with Trish and would call him later, so that we could spend some time together. He has been doing exactly what he said he was going to do, like not being so controlling of my every move. He has been taking his medication and things have been great between us, so I was in a good place right now after finally being able to tell my best friends that we were back together. I've been spending some of my free time with Kylief's mom and she's a sweetheart, and I've been enjoying getting to know the woman who birthed the man that I was in love with. I remember Kenya telling me that his mother tried to warn her sister, but she never said anything negative about her son to me, only voicing that she was glad he was back on the right track. Her health was a little better, but Kylief still had an aide working part-time just to help with meals, medication, and appointments when needed.

After leaving the restaurant, we ran into Toni and she was with Kylief's ex-girlfriend, Demayo, causing me to roll my eyes. I couldn't help but release an exasperated breath, to just keep it moving without going upside her damn head. Toni looked like she was about to deliver any day now, because her stomach was huge and her wobble game was strong.

"Hey, you guys," Toni sang like she was happy to see us.

Since she's been pregnant we have been cordial, and I guess that had to do with her not feeling that I was a threat anymore. Some females swear that once they get pregnant by a man, all the issues that they once stressed about are no longer, because they just know that the man will never leave them now that a baby is on the way. She said that she was just leaving her doctor appointment and I wanted to ask her why wasn't Tristian ~~wasn't~~ with her. I also wanted to ask her how did she know the bird that was clucking behind her. She had to know her well for her to be going to her doctor's appointment with her in replacement of Tristian.

"I'm sorry for being rude, this is my coworker and friend, Demayo," she apologized, but nobody was checking for that bitch.

"No problem; your friend and I already encountered a physical introduction," I said, looking Demayo up and down with a frown on my face.

"Is that the girl that ran up on you?" Trish asked getting in defense mode, ready to throw down if needed.

"Yes, it is but trust; she will not be trying to run into this brick wall again." I let it be known that she's wasn't stupid enough to try that shit again.

"Whoa, what's going on?" Toni asked, rubbing her belly unaware that her friend got her ass kicked over a man that no longer belongs to her.

"Nothing is going on, it's just once upon a time ago your girl ran up on me, because she's the ex to my current boyfriend," I clarified.

"Ky likes to refer to me as ex so that he could continue doing him, but trust, the only thing that changed was my title. If you want to believe that I'm no longer in his life, that's on you because I'm not here to convince you otherwise," Demayo sassed with a roll of her eyes.

"That's fine, because I'm not about to sit here and entertain what you believe, because if he cared about you, he wouldn't have left your ass on that ground. Trish, let's be out

185

and Toni, be careful of the company you keep," I said, pulling Trish along before shit went all the way left. I wanted so bad to put hands on her, but it wouldn't have made sense to be fighting over a man who already belonged to me. If she felt that she was more to him then he claims was between the two of them; that was on her, because he wasn't claiming her ass to me, so we were good. These bitches need to realize that if that man's only claiming you behind closed doors and not out in the streets, he's not your man. And they damn sure shouldn't be fighting for a title that doesn't belong to them.

Chapter Twenty-Two
Demayo

I stood in my condo located on the lower eastside, peering down through my bay windows and fuming inside. Kylief told me that he wasn't with Jess anymore, so I needed his ass here to explain to me why he lied to me. Fifteen minutes into pacing back and forth, he was finally at my door and I couldn't wait to get in his ass.

"What the fuck did I tell you about blowing up my shit?" he barked as soon as he walked through the door.

"I thought you said that you weren't fucking with Jess anymore?" I questioned, not about to let him intimidate me.

I watched him as his jaw tightened and out of frustration, he rubbed the stubble on his face that needed to be shaved the hell off, but I didn't care. I was tired of being his doormat when he couldn't even keep it real with me.

"Demayo, stay in your lane," he warned.

"What lane would that be because you have me in so many, but none of those lanes benefit me and I'm sick of it. All

187

you do is sell me bullshit just to get me to do shit for you, but you don't give a shit about me," I snapped.

"Any fucking thing you do for me you get compensated, so miss me with that bullshit you got coming out of your mouth."

"Compensated, but at what cost? I have bent over backwards for your ass, only for you to make me fall in love with you, thinking you felt the same way about me. Do you think that I would have done half the shit I've done for you, if I didn't feel that you loved me the same as I loved you? I just don't understand how you could give to someone else, what you should have given to me," I yelled.

"Let's be clear about a few things, because I think that you may have forgotten how this shit between us even started. I'm going to give you a chance to correct me if I'm wrong, but were you not a fucking runner for Twin when we first met? When that nigga got killed and you had no fucking means to pay your fucking bills, did you not beg me to let you make drops for me? Yes, we started fucking around and fucking around led to you being with me longer than I expected the shit to last, but don't you ever fix your face like this was some love affair that we were having. I'm not saying that I have no feelings for you because if I didn't, I wouldn't have stopped you from doing you or moved you in with me, but the shit just didn't work and I need you to understand that and move the fuck on," he finished.

"First off, I didn't beg you for shit; you approached me with the proposition and I accepted, because it was what I was doing and I needed the money. You're the one who stepped to me, wanting to be with me and I didn't have a problem with it, because I was feeling you. So, when you said that since I was your girl, you didn't want me to be transporting packages and moved me in with you, *that's* how the shit got started. So, no; I'm not the one that got shit twisted, it's you. If I had continued to play nice and not complained about you out in the streets all times of the night, fucking other bitches we will still be together. None of that is important right now, because it has nothing to do with what I'm asking you about. It's like you're beating around the bush, when all I want to know is why you lied and said that you were no longer with her anymore."

"I'm going to clear this shit up for you, even though I don't feel I owe you an explanation. When I told you that we weren't together anymore, it's because we weren't, but we just decided to give it another chance. So, I'm going to need you to fall back whenever you see her and stop making it seem like I'm with you, because we are not together."

"And how do you suggest I do that when you keep giving me mixed signals that you want to be with me, when it's convenient for you? If you're done with me, then be done and do not keep fucking with my emotions like I don't have feelings," I stressed, trying not to release the tears that were threatening to fall.

"I'm done," he said, with finality in his voice and those tears fell, because I knew that he was really done this time.

I'm not going to lie and say it didn't hurt, because it hurts like hell that I kept being the fool for him, only for him to leave me again. You would think that since I was the one that knew all his secrets, and never judged his ass no matter what; he would think twice about doing me dirty, but I guess not. Why should I continue to be loyal to someone who isn't loyal to me? He fucked with the wrong female's feelings this time and he will get what's coming to him, the same way Twin got his. Twin also thought that playing with my feelings was the move, but he quickly realized that I wasn't that bitch. These niggas think that just because a bitch's out here on a side hustle that I was cool being treated like a side hoe, but that was far from the case and I didn't take lightly to being played like one.

I refused to make eye contact with him as he stood to leave, because being weak was foreign to me, but he always brought it out of me. I honestly believed that my being that strong individual and not taking shit from anyone was what attracted him to me. Once I fell in love with him, it was like that brick wall that I had up and that "I don't give a fuck" attitude just came crashing down when it came to him. I was never the needy or clingy type when it came to any dude, not needing them for anything, because I always did what I had to do to get mine. He changed me and I thought it was for the better, but it wasn't. All it did was make me vulnerable and feel like I couldn't live without him. After locking the door behind him, I rushed back over to the table that I left my phone on, because it was ringing.

"Hey, Toni," I said, after answering the call.

"Hey, girl. I was just calling to check on you," she responded.

"He just left and I swear, I hate the day that I met his ass, because he doesn't give a shit about how I feel. He doesn't understand that I was good without him pursuing me, just to make me love him only to do me like this. I promise you that he's the only nigga that I gave my heart to, because I never trusted any nigga and once I decide to, this is what happens," I vented.

"You can't blame yourself for stepping out of your comfort zone and falling in love, because you had no idea that it would end like this. He's to blame for stringing you along, knowing that he wasn't feeling you quite as much as you were feeling him. As much as I want to say that Jess played a part in this, I can honestly say that this is all him, because she had no idea of the extent of you two's relationship. You know for a fact that I never liked her ass because of the relationship that she and Tristian has, but I had to learn that she owed me nothing. All the energy that I put into not liking her, I should have put that same energy into his ass and once I realized that, I gave his ass an ultimatum and we been good since. All I wanted from him was for him to involve me when it came to her, if they were only friends like they claimed to be. But in your case, it seems that he played on your emotions, knowing that he didn't really want to be in a relationship with you. I know you probably don't want to hear any of this, but I think that you should just let go and let him be, Demayo. I'm not trying to be all up in your business, all I'm trying to do is be there for you like you've always been there for me, giving me advice," she expressed.

Chapter Twenty-Three
Jess

I walked into the police station not really wanting to be here, but Trish talked me into coming to speak to the detective that was handling the case. She just kept stressing that I needed to let the detective know of the conversation that I had with Kenya the night she was murdered. Things were going really good with Kylief and I didn't want to mess that up by going behind his back, but if it meant getting Trish off my back, then so be it.

"Can I please speak with the detective that's handling the case regarding Kenya Harris?" I asked the officer behind the desk.

After giving my name and stating that I had information regarding the case, I was asked to have a seat and told that someone would be out to speak to me. I waited for about twenty minutes, before I was being called back to the front desk by the officer that assisted me earlier.

"So, you're going to go up those stairs and turn left and it will be the last door on the right, where Detective Smalls will be waiting for you," he instructed.

As I walked up the stairs, my nerves started to get the best of me and I started to curse myself for allowing Trish to talk me into coming to the damn police station. Walking into the office, I noticed that Detective Smalls was a woman and not a man like I expected. She was dressed in some navy slacks, a white blouse and a navy-blue blazer, with long dreads hanging from her roots, and just from her stance I could tell that she was a dyke. Her sexuality didn't bother me; it was just something that I did when I was nervous and trying to calm my nerves.

"How may I help you?" she spoke sharply as if I was interrupting her from whatever she had going on before I entered her office.

"I-I have some information about K-Kenya Harris," I stuttered nervously.

"And what might that information be and how do you know the victim?" she asked and I tried my hardest not to feel intimidated by her intense stare, but I was.

I didn't trust the police because they had a way of twisting people's words and my admission to being the last person to speak with Kenya might land my ass as a suspect. So yes, I was very intimidated at this point and prayed that she didn't think I had something to do with her death, once she heard what I had to say.

"I didn't know Ms. Harris; in fact I just met her the night of her death, because she approached me asking if she could speak to me about my boyfriend, Kylief—"

"Kylief James?" she interrupted.

"Yes," I responded.

"Ok, continue," she said, tapping her pen against her notepad, really making me nervous now.

"I agreed to talk to her, being that she said that it was about Kylief, so I met with her at a diner that was about a block from where she approached me. She basically told me that she wanted to warn me to leave Kylief alone, because he was abusive to her sister and that she believed he was responsible for her death. Her reason for giving me that information was because she said she wished that someone would have warned her sister, so she was trying to save my life. I thanked her for the information and we went our separate ways and I was in shock to see on the news the next morning she was found dead in her car. I know that I should have come in sooner with this information and to be honest, I was scared to involve myself, but I knew that I had to come in and do the right thing if it might help find her murderer," I finished, hoping that she believed me.

"Ms. Johnson, I appreciate you coming down here to speak with someone, but it seems as Kenya left out quite a few details when speaking of Kylief," she informed me, leaving me curious as to what she was speaking of, so I waited for her to continue.

"Kenya failed to mention that she was seeing Kylief behind her sister's back and that a few days before her sister's death, they both were arrested. Someone at the family home called about a physical confrontation between the two sisters, caused by Serena confronting Kenya about having a relationship with Kylief. When Selena's body was found days after the confrontation, Kenya was brought in for questioning, where she pointed the finger at Kylief, stating that he was abusing her sister. She also denied having a relationship with him, so he too was brought in for questioning, but we didn't have enough evidence to prove that either one of them was responsible for her death. I honestly have no idea why she approached you, other than she may have still been seeing Kylief, and wanted you to leave him alone. I appreciate you coming in and if you have anything that you forgot to mention or have any questions, feel free to give me a call," she said, handing me her card.

I felt like she was now rushing me up out of her office, but I was happy that she was dismissing me. I just knew that she was going to ask me about my whereabouts the night Kenya was murdered. Though, I could have assured her that I was not out killing nobody the night that I just buried my father and Mama Bear. I left the police station in a daze about all that I learned. Kylief seemed to have left out a whole lot when he called himself being honest about his relationship with Serena. I wasn't going to say anything to him about what I learned because I didn't even want him to know that I went down to the police station. What I did want to do was find out what he was doing at my job that day and what his relationship is with my boss, being that he was able to call and get information about me. I thought his knowing my boss had something to do with him being his lawyer, but now I wasn't too sure, because he hasn't been back to the office. Also, the day that he called my boss to ask about me, it seemed to be more of a personal relationship between the two of them.

I didn't even mention to him that I ran into his ex-girlfriend again and that she's friends with my best friend, Tristian's girl, but now I don't even know if I wanted to have any conversations with him. I feel like I needed to put my guard back up with him, since he failed to share everything with me and pray that he didn't have anything to do with anyone's death. I didn't want to be his next victim if he was in fact responsible for Serena and Kenya's deaths, so I knew for sure that I was keeping my visit to the police station to myself. I thought about everything as I got into my car and headed towards my job. The wheels in my head were spinning, because I didn't know what the truth was anymore when it came to Kylief, but I was going to try and find out some truth on my own.

I sat in my car until the time on the dashboard read a quarter to six, before getting out of the car and heading inside. I knew the only person that would be there was my co-worker, Charles, but I wasn't worried, because he wasn't a snitch. I used my keycard to get on the elevator, a privilege that only a few of us had after hours, because we stayed overtime sometimes. Charles was a paralegal, so he was always working overtime, because he always wanted to make sure that the lawyers had what they needed before they needed it. Walking in, I saw him going over some files and when he noticed me, he walked over to me offering his condolences. I told him that I just had to grab something from Luke's office and that I wouldn't be longer than a few minutes.

Once in Luke's office, I had no idea what I was looking for, so I just started going through files in his file cabinet, but nothing caught my eye that was related to Kylief. I started getting frustrated, because I'd now been searching for about twenty minutes and still had nothing, until I noticed a box under his desk marked "confidential". I pulled the box out, just to find that you needed a combination just to open it, so I was pissed now that I wasted my time coming down here and leaving empty-handed. I said goodnight to Charles, asking him not to mention that I stopped by the office, which he agreed like I knew he would.

I was still staying at my place, but this was my last week there, because I would be officially moved into the house I grew up in this weekend. When I pulled up to my house, Tristian's car was parked out front and I couldn't contain the smile that formed on my face, even though I tried. We have since made up, but we haven't been spending any time together and that was foreign to us, but it was because our relationship has become strained. I don't know if strained is the word to use, so I'll just say that it has become awkward, knowing that we crossed the friendship line, but I just want my friend back. I needed him right now, because he has always been my go-to person when I was dealing with shit, and Lord knows I need him with the shit I'm dealing with now.

I grabbed my phone and bag before getting out of the car, biting my bottom lip because that was the only way to contain my smile.

"Hey you," he said.

"Hey," I said, not making eye contact, walking to the front door to open it.

I tried to erase the thoughts of him that was floating around in my head right now, but it was hard because his cologne triggered them. Once inside, he went to his favorite spot on the couch and I tried my best to just act normal as I took a seat across from him.

"So, how have you been?" I asked him, finally making eye contact.

"Chilling," he said, saying no more.

"So, you just chilling? Are you excited that your baby about to be born?" I asked, trying to get him to say more than what he was saying.

"I'm anxious to know if it's a boy or girl, but I don't want to talk about that. What's been going on with you?" he said, now staring at me intensely.

He had me thinking that he stopped by because Toni mentioned what happened between me and her little friend. I wasn't about to go there with him because if she was still with Kylief, she wouldn't feel the need to come at me, trying to prove it to me. She was a dead issue for me unless I caught them together, so in the words of Evelyn Lozada, she's a non-motherfucking factor.

"I'm good, but I miss our friendship because after we both said that we were going to do better, you still seem distant. I'm used to either talking to you or seeing you every day, but that hasn't been the case. I know that the only reason you showed up is probably because Toni mentioned seeing me at the restaurant, and what happened at the restaurant with her friend," I said, not about to pretend like I didn't know why he showed up here.

"So, I'm not supposed to worry about you anymore?" he barked and I rolled my eyes at his putting words in my mouth.

"I didn't say that you're not supposed to worry about me. I'm just saying that if Toni didn't mention anything to you, you wouldn't be here right now."

"How the hell am I supposed to be with you or calling you all the time when you're with that nigga? You say you missed me, but I'm just a phone call away if you want to talk to me or even to ask me to come through. But that call never comes, so don't blame me for not being here," he said, making a point but I was waiting on him to call me.

"That's not true, Tristian, and whether you want to believe it or not, it's not a day that goes by that I don't be wanting you to be here, sitting in your favorite spot on my couch. I miss you and I want you to know that just because I'm with someone else, it doesn't mean that we had to stop being friends. I be wanting to call you and ask you to come through, but I be trying to be respectful of your relationship with Toni. No, I never cared before how much time you spent over here when she was home, but she's with child now," I told him.

"So, if that's how you feel, then why blame me for why we stopped spending time together, Jess, because I'm not a mind reader. If you want me to come over, all you have to do is call me and I promise you I'll be here. Now that we are on the subject, I just want to say that I'm sorry about how I've been treating you with my words. I'm jealous of the relationship that you have with him, because of the feelings that I have for you. You always respected my relationship with Toni, no matter how much you disliked her and I just feel that I should have done the same. I know that what happened between us shouldn't have happened, because had we not been vulnerable that night, I believe you wouldn't have given in, so I do feel like I took advantage of the situation," he admitted.

I just looked at him before responding, because he had to know that I have loved his ass from the first time we were old enough to know what a feeling for the opposite sex was. If only he knew that I wanted that night to happen, just as much as he wanted it to and the only reason it never happened before was because I was respecting his relationship. I just wished that I had the courage that his mother and my father had to admit the love that they had for one another and act on it. Even though they didn't get to spend the rest of their lives together, at least they got to share the love that they had for one another, and died knowing that they loved each other.

I'm not going to lie and say that I don't love Kylief, but he has too much unknown baggage and I had no idea if I wanted to stay with him. I could deal with an ex-girlfriend who couldn't let go, but all these scenarios surrounding murder had me kind of shook, and it's just a matter of telling him how I feel about it.

Chapter Twenty-Four
Tristian

I sat on the couch, admiring Jess' beauty as she was lost in whatever she had on her mind that distracted her from responding to me. I didn't know what she had going on, but I did know that she shouldn't be dealing with nothing other than the death of her father. I know she cares for dude, but the fact that he isn't here with her says a lot about him. I'm pissed at myself for not putting our differences to the side and just be here for her. We used to be able to talk to each other about anything, so the fact that she was holding in whatever was going on with her, I know it had to do with me. Since she got with dude, anytime she tried to tell me what she was feeling or just talk to me about him, I would always shut her down, so that needed to change. It was just that I cared for her and didn't want to hear anything that had to do with him, but if I wanted to be that friend that I always been, that shit was going to have to change.

"Are you ok?" I decided to break the trance that she was in.

"I'm good, just thinking about something, but to respond to what you were saying, I don't think that you need to blame yourself for what happened between us. If I didn't want it to happen, trust me; it wouldn't have happened so stop blaming yourself. Also, I want you to know that you were right about my having feelings for you, the same feelings that you have for me. I always lied about having feelings for you, because you were with Toni and I wasn't trying to get hurt," she said, as she sucked on her bottom lip to stop it from trembling, because this is the first time that she ever expressed having feelings for me.

"When are you going back to work?" I asked her.

"Probably next week, why?" she asked.

"Go upstairs and pack a bag," I told her.

"Tristian, we are not teenagers anymore where we could just up and go away, and did you forget that you have a baby due possibly any day now?" she reminded me, but I didn't care.

"Go pack a bag, Jess, and let me worry about that," I smiled to reassure her that we could do this just like old times.

When we were in high school, we used to always leave the city for a few days just to get away, and we would never take Trish with us. She used to say that Jess liked me more than her, but that was never the case; Jess and I just had a different type of friendship, the one where we cared about each other but never acted on it. When my mother got me my first car at the age of seventeen, it was the best gift that she could have ever gotten me, because that was how I got to spend most of my time with Jess. Even if it was me calling her up to ride to the store with me, it meant that I was going to be in her presence. So, if only for a day or two, I wanted to take her away to be in her presence again without any distractions. When I say distractions, I mean her boyfriend and my girlfriend, but she didn't need to know that because if she did, she probably wouldn't have agreed to go. She went upstairs to pack a bag but when she came back downstairs, I didn't understand why she was carrying such a big bag, when I just told her that we were only going to be gone for a day or two.

"What the hell did you pack, when I just told you that we were only going to be gone for a day or two," I laughed.

"It's the bag that makes it look like it's a lot, but it's not a lot," she smirked as I reached around her, grabbing the bag and pretending that I could barely lift it, causing her to laugh.

"Do you think we should call Trish and let her know where we're going because the last time I spoke to her, I was headed to the police station. I don't want her to think that I was locked up if she doesn't hear from me," she asked me.

"Police station?" I questioned.

"Long story," she sighed deeply.

"Well, call her to let her know that you made it back home and that you will call her later with details. We have a long drive, so your long story will be perfect to tell as we drive off into the sunset," I joked.

"Ok, I'll call her, but you need to call Toni and tell her something too," she suggested.

"What about your dude, shouldn't you be calling him to tell him something?" I fired back.

"He'll be alright, any questions that need to be answered, I will answer when I get back," she said and I left it at that, because I couldn't care less if she called him or not.

"So, spill, why you were at the police station?" I said to her once we were in the car.

She must have thought I forgot about the shit that fast, because she sucked her teeth like she didn't want to tell me. If I had to call Trish and make her ass tell me, that's what I was prepared to do, because one of them was going to tell me something. I turned to see her taking a deep breath before I focused back on the road, waiting for her to tell me.

"Ok, so you remember my telling Trish about the female that approached me and how she was killed that same night, right? So, your sister, refusing to leave well enough alone, convinced me to go down to the police station and tell them about the conversation that I had with the girl. I didn't get to go the day that she told me to go, because Kylief showed up at my front door, demanding that I take a ride with him. I'm not going to lie and say that I wasn't afraid, because I was. I thought that he was trying to kidnap me or some shit, but it turned out that he didn't want to kidnap me. He just wanted to explain to me what was causing his actions as far as his erratic behavior and since we were talking and being honest, I told him about what the girl, Kenya, said. So, after talking to him, I still felt the need to let the authorities know about the conversation that I had with her, because I didn't want anything to come back to me, so that's where I was coming back from today. Anyway, after I spoke with a Detective Smalls and mentioned Kylief's name, she went on to tell me that the day before Kenya's sister was killed; Kenya and her sister had a fight because the sister found out that Kenya was sleeping with Kylief. She said that Kylief and Kenya both were questioned for the sister's murder, but it wasn't enough evidence to charge either of them," she finished and I'm not going to lie, I was pissed.

"This nigga got a whole fucking soap opera going on and you need to let his ass go, before you get caught up in some bullshit. I know you don't want to see me behind bars, so it's best you leave his ass alone. Just because they didn't find any evidence to convict him, that doesn't mean that he didn't do it." I barked because I just felt like she was taking this shit lightly, and I needed for her to understand how important it was to stop fucking with him.

"I already know what I have to do, Tristian, and trust me; it's going to get done," she said, but I didn't know if she was going to follow through this time, after saying that shit before and doing the opposite by staying with his ass.

No more words were spoken as I cruised the rest of to the way to Atlantic City with the music blaring. I was trying to calm myself down because like I said; I was pissed but not at that nigga, I was pissed at her ass. I didn't give a fuck if that bitch, Kenya, was selling her ass a dream or not, but after hearing some shit like that, she had no business riding with that nigga anywhere. I know that love or lust; whatever she wants to call it, can make you do some stupid shit, but she just put her life at risk if that shit happened to be true. I was also pissed because she confided in Trish and not me, the person who she always confided in when it came to these knucklehead niggas, but now I guess she didn't feel comfortable telling me everything anymore.

I pulled up to the Borgata Hotel, not believing that I haven't been back here in so long, because this used to be our spot. I swear, the stress just melted away as soon as I handed my keys to the valet and I loved how Jess' face was lit up right now, because she needed this time away just as much as I did. I didn't tell her but the reservations were made before I even got her to agree to come with me, but she didn't need to know that. I wasn't a gambler, so being here was just to get some away time with her, and I was going to try to enjoy it without bringing her bitch-ass man up again. Toni has been blowing my phone up but I wasn't going to return her call just yet, because we just got here so I didn't want any negativity tonight. I knew that she wasn't in labor because if she had been, she would have had everyone and their mother trying to get in touch with me.

"I'm going to go take a shower," she said, once we made it to the room.

I waited a good five minutes before I stripped out of my clothes to go join her in the shower and I wasn't trying to hear her shutting me down. I stepped into the shower and she immediately tried covering her body.

"Tristian, what are you doing? I didn't come here for this, I just came to get away," her mouth said, but her facial expression said something else as she stared at my manhood.

She turned her back on me, so I eased up on her and grabbed her from behind, whispering in her ear and telling her to just relax. I turned her around to face me and she was shivering and I didn't know if it was from her being cold or nervous.

"Jess, it's ok," I said, pulling her into me.

"I'm scared," she said just above a whisper as a few tears fell.

I knew exactly what she was feeling, because she always told me that she was scared to fall in love out of fear of losing that person. She fell in love with Kylief and this happened and now she finally got the nerve to tell me how she really felt, knowing that I belonged to someone else. She was probably thinking that she could never have me as her own.

She didn't have her father anymore so I know that she was feeling alone, like she doesn't have anyone right now. I just wanted her to know that I love her and that nothing was going to change that, not even Toni being pregnant with my seed.

"Don't be scared, Jess, because you have me and I'm not going anywhere," I told her, wiping her tears away before kissing her deeply.

Chapter Twenty-Five
Jess

I was sitting up in the middle of the hotel's big ass, king size bed, watching Tristian sleep as he snored lightly. He was so perfect to me and I wished that we didn't have to go back, because once we go back, my fairytale romance is going to come to an end. The things he did to my body last night as he made love to me had me letting go of everything that I held onto all these years. As much as I wanted to just say fuck Toni and her being pregnant with his baby, I couldn't because it wouldn't be right. He stirred in his sleep before opening his eyes, now staring at me with a smirk on his handsome face.

"You good?" he asked, just as his phone rang. "Hold that thought, pretty lady," he said before answering the call.

"I'm out of town, so I'm going to need you to go up there and stay with her until I get there," he said into the phone.

When he ended the call, he kissed my lips before telling me that Toni was in labor and that Trish was going to stay with her until he got there. There was nothing else to be said, so I got my things packed and after getting dressed, we headed back to the city. By the time we pulled up to North Shore Hospital, it was going on six in the morning and I felt bad, because Trish called about an hour ago to tell him she left the hospital just as Toni started to push. He said that Toni's people was up there tripping, so Trish said she got kicked out of the hospital because she was going to fuck Toni's mother up. I couldn't tell how Tristian felt about possibly missing the birth of his firstborn because his face held no emotion. I did begin to worry if he was upset with me, because had we not been in Atlantic City, he would have been here with her.

"I'm going to call an Uber," I said, getting out of the car.

"Nah, you don't have to do that; I'll take you home," he said, taking my hand and pulling me with him.

"So, is this why you couldn't be here to see your fucking daughter born?" I heard someone scream as soon as we got off the elevator on the labor and delivery floor.

Tristian now wore a smile on his face at the sound of him having a daughter, ignoring the woman as I told him congratulations. I didn't realize that we were still holding hands, so I let go of his hand because it was disrespectful, but he grabbed my hand back, telling me that it was ok.

"I tried to tell my daughter that you weren't shit and that you were sleeping with your 'so-called best friend'," the woman continued who I now knew as Toni mother.

"I'm trying not to disrespect you because you're Toni's mom, but I'm going to need you to get the fuck up out of my face," he finally snapped.

I put both hands on his face in a calming manner, causing him to look at me, because I didn't want him flying off the handle and end up going to jail for hitting one of her family members.

"Listen, I'm going to call Uber, so go and see your daughter," I told him because I already felt like shit that he missed the delivery because he was with me.

"Look, I already know what you're thinking, so stop thinking it. It's not your fault and although I would have liked to be here for the birth, I wasn't and that's on me. Text me when you make it home safely, ok? I love you," he said, kissing my lips like we were the only two people in the waiting room.

Her family was going in after seeing him kiss me on my lips, but he ignored them, walking me to the elevator and telling me to get home safe. He repeated for me to make sure that I text him as soon as I made it into the house. As soon as I got outside to wait for my Uber, I saw Kylief leaning up against his truck, wearing a scowl on his face. I knew that Demayo called his ass, because I peeped her sitting in the corner of the waiting area, but decided not to acknowledge her.

"So, is this the reason you couldn't answer your phone?" he barked.

I swear, I didn't feel like dealing with this right now, after having such an enjoyable time with Tristian. Now I wished that I had punched that bitch, Demayo, in her face when I saw her sitting there with a smirk on her damn face. She didn't have to worry about trying to get me caught up anymore, because if she wants him, she could have him.

"I see your little girlfriend called you to tell you that I was here," I said, with a roll of my eyes.

"It doesn't matter who told me that you were here, because my only concern is why are you here and why aren't you answering any of my calls?"

"So, I'm not supposed to be here when my best friend's baby is being born?" I asked with attitude dripping from my question.

"Let's go, because I'm not about to be out here arguing with you, when you know that the nigga wasn't even here for his baby's birth," he said, opening the passenger side door, but I hesitated because Tristian told me to stay away from him.

"I called Uber already," I voiced sternly.

"Fuck Uber, Jess, and get in the fucking car," he shouted, making me wonder if he was still taking his medication.

I didn't want him to make a scene, so I just got into the car soaking it up to my need to talk to him to let him know that it was over. We drove to his house in silence, which was fine because I didn't want to argue with his ass anyway. I just wanted to speak my piece and end this shit on a good note, and call my Uber back and take my ass home. I'm already going to be charged for a ride that I didn't even get to take, being that I didn't call to cancel the car. When we got to his house, I stormed into the living room ready to get this talk over with, but he felt the need to interrogate me first, which wasn't even necessary.

"What's going on with you and that nigga? Is that the reason him and his goons came here and kicked my ass, because you're fucking him?" he asked with spittle flying into my face and in that moment, I realized that I fucked up getting in his damn car.

"No, I'm not fucking him and as far as him coming here, I know nothing about it," I lied and he knew that I was lying, but at this point I didn't care.

He didn't say anything to me about it when it happened, so I didn't need to hear about it now and if he had an issue, he should have taken it up with Tristian. If he'd kept his hands to himself, he wouldn't have gotten a visit from Tristian and his goons, as he called them.

"Well, standing in a hospital kissing that nigga says something different," he stated, pacing the floor like a madman.

"Look Kylief, that's not even important right now, because this relationship isn't working for me anymore. I don't want to fight with you about it, so I'm just going to call my Uber so that I could go home," I told him.

"Now you don't want to be with me? I thought we just had this conversation and we agreed to be together. So, what changed?"

How about you still sleeping with your big-headed, ex-girlfriend, Demayo, or if that isn't enough, how about I believe you to be a fucking liar when you failed to share that you were sleeping with Kenya? I wanted to say but I didn't, because all that would have done was cause him to probably go upside my head.

My phone started to ring and I knew that it was Tristian, because he had his own personal ringtone in my phone. I didn't text him when I got here, so now he was probably worried about me; I needed to find a way to text him.

"I need to use the bathroom," I said to Kylief.

"I don't have a problem with you using the bathroom, but leave your phone here because you're not about to disrespect my crib to talk to that nigga," he barked.

I didn't have a problem leaving my phone because it had a lock code, but going to the bathroom defeat the purpose if I couldn't use my phone. I didn't want him to know the reason I was going to the bathroom was to use my phone, so I put the phone down on the coffee table before going upstairs to the bathroom.

Once in the bathroom, I cursed myself for coming here, thinking that I would be able to reason with him. I didn't have to use the bathroom, so I just stood there thinking about how I was going getting him to allow me to call an Uber to get up out of here. I didn't even want him to take me back to my place, because once he gets that we're done, I don't want to see his ass ever again. Yes, I still have feelings for him, but my feelings for Tristian are deeper and that's who I want to be with, if he'll have me. I'm tired of caring about everyone else's happiness when I deserve to be happy too, but I want to be happy with a sane man, not one that only can be good to me when he's taking his medication. I flushed the toilet and turned on the sink water, just in case he was standing outside the bathroom door with his crazy ass. After washing my hands, I noticed that there was nothing to dry my hands with, so I went out into the hallway to get a hand towel from the linen closet. I grabbed a towel and something fell out that I tried to pick up quickly and put it back, before he heard the thump that I just made and come upstairs.

As I bent down to pick up the items, my heart stopped momentarily at seeing the watch and wallet that belonged to my father. I didn't want to believe it, but after turning the watch over to see the engraving, I knew that it belonged to my father. I stood frozen at the thought that Kylief was responsible for what happened to my father and Mama Bear, but what reason would he have had to hurt them? He didn't even know them, so why would he go to their home and kill them and in that moment, I started to panic because I didn't have my phone to call anyone. Now, I wasn't too sure about continuing this conversation with him, because my dumb ass didn't peg him for the murder of Kenya, thinking that he wasn't capable. Now I was stuck in this house with him, not knowing if I was going to make it out alive as I stood there shaking not knowing what to do. I heard him coming up the stairs, so I put the watch and wallet back where I found it and pretended like I was just coming out of the bathroom, by the time he made it to the top of the stairs.

"Are you ok? You been up here for a long time," he said, looking at me suspiciously.

"I-I'm not feeling well. I-I think I need to go home," I stuttered nervously.

"Well, if you're not feeling well, why would I drive you all the way home, when you can stay here and rest. Let me grab you a washcloth and towel, so that you could shower and lay down." he said, moving towards the closet.

"No! I'm ok; let's just finish what we were talking about." I panicked, heading towards the stairs and praying he followed me.

I breathe a sigh of relief once I saw him follow me downstairs, but I didn't want to continue with the breaking up conversation I just wanted to go home. I felt sick to my stomach being in the presence of the man who killed my father and not able to do anything about it. I couldn't say anything to him because I knew that I wouldn't make it out alive, so I had to think. I hoped he didn't notice that I was shaking, because that would be a dead giveaway that I saw what he had in the closet. I closed my eyes briefly, silently praying that I got up out of here with my life.

Chapter Twenty-Six
Tristian

When I walked into Toni's room she was wearing a pissed look on her face and she had every right to be pissed. I knew that she wasn't going to go in on me, being that the nurse was still in the room, so I walked over to the baby bassinet where the nurse was attending to her and the smile I was wearing faded. She didn't look anything like me and to be honest, she didn't look anything like Toni's ass either. We both were brown-skinned, but this little girl was a dark complexion. Now I know that looks aren't supposed to determine the paternity of a baby, but this fucking baby wasn't mine. Unlike Toni's ass, I wasn't going to wait until the nurse left before questioning her ass, because I was pissed.

"Who does this fucking baby belong to, Toni?" I barked at her ass.

"What are you talking about, Tristian? Don't fucking play with me because you know this is your baby," she snapped.

"If I knew it was my baby, I wouldn't have just asked you whose fucking baby this was, so stop playing with me and answer my damn question. That baby is fucking burnt skin when we both standing here a whole fucking shade different," I said, causing the nurse to burst out laughing, but apologizing at the same time.

"I can't believe that you missed your daughter birth because you were out frolicking with that bitch, Jess, just to get here and insult my fucking child," she yelled.

"So, you really going to lay there and try and convince me that the baby that's laying in that bassinet is my baby? If that's my baby, you're going to have to prove the shit to me, so holla at one of these fucking nurses and tell them that we want a paternity test done, ASAP."

"I just can't believe you would do this to me, Tristian, because you know I haven't been with anyone else. I guess I'm guilty of something now, just because you were out screwing your 'best friend', when you should have been here with me. How do you think it makes me feel to have just pushed out your fucking baby alone, to get a text telling me that you were here, but showed up with that bitch? Then, you had the audacity to stand out there and kiss that bitch on the lips, like my feelings don't matter. If that's what you want and who you want to be with, then you could have at least had some damn decency when you knew you was coming here," she screamed with a pained look on her face.

She was right; I could have handled the situation better, but her mother pissed me off and I wanted to rub it in her fucking face. After seeing that baby that don't belong to me, I couldn't care less how anybody feels about the way I handled my shit. She just better be lucky I wasn't here to see her push out that fucking tar baby, because I would have flipped the fuck out on her and the motherfucking doctor that helped her push that shit out. When she told me that she was pregnant, I was feeling like the luckiest man in the world to be having my firstborn, so for her to try to trap me with a fucking baby that she knew wasn't mine is fucked up.

"Hit me with a text when you schedule the paternity test," I told her before leaving out of the room, pissed that I had to send Jess home for this bullshit.

Jess and I could have still been laid up in Atlantic City, making love the entire weekend like I planned. I called her phone a few times, but she wasn't answering and I had to remind myself that it was after six in the morning when we got back to the city. She probably was sleeping, so I was going to head on home and get some rest and holla at her when I got up.

I was going to make sure that I got in her ass for not texting me to let me know she made it home, knowing how I worry about her.

I woke up about seven that evening and I still haven't heard from Jess, but I did have a few text messages from Toni, asking me if I was coming back up to the hospital. I wasn't going back up to the hospital, because I will fuck around and kill her ass. I tore that fucking hospital bracelet off my wrist as soon as I got outside of that bitch, so they needed to make another one for the real fucking baby daddy, because it wasn't me. All I needed from her was to schedule the test so that I could be done with her simple ass for good for trying to pin that baby on me. It's always the ones that claim to be so fucking loyal to you that fuck around and do you dirty, but it's all good; I'm not going to sweat it.

I started to worry about Jess, so I called Trish to see if she heard from her, but she said that she hasn't spoken to her since the day before. That would be the night we left to spend some time together, so for her not to reach out to Trish for the tea on why she was going to fight Toni's mom, made me think that something was up.

I showered and changed my clothes before getting in my car, driving to her house to see if she was home. Her car was parked, but she wasn't home and from the looks of it, she hasn't been home, so I was wondering if she was with that fuck nigga. That would explain why she wasn't answering any of my calls or text messages, but I was going to give her the benefit of the doubt because she could have crashed at her pop's house. I was going to go see Trish and let her know what happened at the hospital and go by Jess' pops crib tonight and her ass better be there or I'm going to be showing up at that nigga's door. I made a stop to get something to eat before heading toward my mom's crib, making sure to pick something up for Trish's ass but when I got there, she had already had a spread cooked for her and her dude. I met him a few times and he seemed like a cool dude, but I've never seen him here at my mom's crib before, so I was feeling some kind of way because he never came when she was living.

"What's up? Did you hear from Jess since I called?" I asked her after putting my takeout from Outback on the table.

"No, I been calling her but she's not answering, and it's not like her not to answer her phone," she said. So, I knew for a fact that when I left, I was going by her pop's crib.

"Why you not up at the hospital?" she asked me.

"I was there, but Toni's ass must have thought I was Stevie Wonder and wouldn't be able to see that her baby wasn't mine," I told her.

"What do you mean, the baby isn't yours? Did you have a test done, because I'm not understanding how you know it's not yours?" she said, looking at me like I was bugging.

"Listen, she's a pretty little girl, but she has the skin tone of an Oreo cookie without the cream," I told her, causing her to laugh.

"I don't mean to laugh, but you can't fix your face to say that's she's not yours, because of her skin color. How are you going to feel if you take a test and she's your daughter and you just called her an Oreo cookie without the cream?" she said, shaking her head.

"Well, after the test…if she's mine, which I highly doubt; I will apologize and kiss her all over her chocolate face for not being there," I chuckled, knowing that it wasn't going to happen, because she's not mine.

"You ain't shit, but I tell you this if security didn't get me up out of that hospital, I was going to fuck her mother up. When I say that they were going in on you, they were going in and to be honest, I could understand how they were feeling. I would have felt the same way if I was a mother seeing my daughter in pain and the daddy wasn't there, but when she started the name calling, I had enough. Then she had the nerve to ask me why the fuck was I even there, acting like I didn't know where you were, so I lost it. Anyway, where the hell was you when you knew that girl was due to deliver any day?" she said now questioning me.

"I took Jess to Atlantic City to get away from everything and everybody for just for a couple of days, praying that Toni didn't go into labor," I admitted.

"Well damn, and you couldn't tell me?" she said.

"Nope, because your ass would have told her not to do it, with your hating ass," I joked.

"Nah, but on some real shit; it was a last-minute thing that I decided and to be honest, I didn't even think she would have agreed. Enough of my business, why that nigga here when he didn't even visit when Mom was alive," I wanted to know, since she was all up in my shit.

"For your our-information, it wasn't like he didn't want to come and meet Mom; it was all me and I regret it now that she didn't get a chance to meet him. He's here because since Mom's passing, I just haven't felt right being away, so if he wanted to see me he had to come here and I offered to cook," she said, mushing me in the back of the head before taking her baked pork chops out of the oven.

"Well, I'm about to smash my food, then I'm going to go and check on Jess, because I'm starting to worry that she's with that abusive nigga again," I told her.

"Do you want me and Mekhi to go with you?" she asked seriously.

"Nah, I'm good and did you forget, I have my own niggas to make a run with me if needed," I said, shutting her down.

"Whatever...just make sure you don't get your ass in trouble if she is with him willingly," she said, but she knew me better than that.

If I have to run up in his crib whether she's there willingly or not, trust; that's what I was going to do and she will be leaving with me. If he had a problem with it, then his ass was going to get dealt with and fuck whatever consequences came with it.

Chapter Twenty-Seven
Tani

I refused all visits today because I was pissed at the world, being that Tristian wasn't trying to claim my child and basically embarrassed me in front of the nurse. Just as I was about to breastfeed my daughter, my room door opened and if I had a fucking gun, I would have shot the person that just walked through the door. He was the reason that I was going through this shit right now, so I hated the ground that carried his weight, instead of cracking and sending his ass straight to hell.

"Why are you here?" I snapped, trying to cover up my breast as much as I could without interrupting my daughter's feeding.

"Now why would you ask a stupid question like that, when you know that I'm here to see my child?" he snarled, walking over to the bed and staring down at her.

"Luke, you're not the father of my child, so I'm going to need for you to leave. Now!" I shouted, causing my breast to fall out of my daughter's mouth and her to start whining.

I swear, I regret the day that I solicited his services as I thought back on the day that I met the devil in human form.

I had just gotten off work, thinking about my conversation with my mother, when she was telling me about seeing Tristian and Jess at Junior's. I was also thinking about how he played me by making me think that he came home with that movie for him and me to watch, so I wasn't in a good place. I remember trying to call him so if I could see if we were good, but he wasn't answering any of my calls or my numerous text messages, pissing me off. The tears fell from my eyes from frustration of not being able to get him on the phone. As I was walking to my car and attempting to send him another text message, I bumped into someone because I wasn't paying attention. That someone turned out to be Luke. If I knew then what I know now, I would have kept it moving.

"I'm sorry," I apologized.

"No problem. Are you ok?" he asked me, but I didn't respond. "A pretty lady such as yourself shouldn't be crying. Are you sure everything is ok?" he tried again.

He was an older gentleman that looked to be in his early forties, so I took that into consideration that maybe he wasn't coming on to me, but genuinely concerned.

"I'm fine, just having an unpleasant day," I responded, just hoping he'd let me be.

"Do you want to talk about it? I'm a good listener," he smiled and I thought about it before agreeing to talk to him, because he looked like the type that wasn't going to give up.

I basically told him what was going on in my relationship with Tristian and he was giving me good advice. I felt comfortable talking to him, because like I said; he was an older gentleman, sort of like a father figure, until the conversation took on as him offering to help me with my relationship.

"So, since you feel like your boyfriend is spending too much time with his 'so-called best friend', what you need to do is form a distraction," he said, leaving me looking at him with a confused look on my face.

"A distraction?" I inquired.

"Yes, if she's spending all her free time with your boyfriend, then you have to find someone to occupy her time. So, if you agree, I'm willing to help you with that distraction." he said.

234

When I gave him Jess' full name, he had a smile on his face confusing me once again, until he told me that my problem worked for him at his law firm. Now, I started getting leery thinking maybe my bumping into him wasn't random, but he assured me that I could trust him.

So, Jess' meeting Luke's brother from another mother, Kylief, wasn't because he admired her from afar; he was there as a favor to Luke. I had no idea that Kylief was going to fall for her and start a relationship with her. I also didn't know that he was Demayo's ex-boyfriend, until the encounter that they had the other day. Anyway, once Jess and Kylief started dating, my relationship was somewhat better and that's when Luke begun threatening me, saying that I owed him. My being naïve, thought that he wanted me to pay him for his services monetarily, but that wasn't the case; he wanted me to sleep with him. At first, I told him that I wasn't going to sleep with him, because I didn't ask him to do this for me. He took it a step further, pretending like he cared for me and only wanted to take me out to dinner, saying that I didn't owe him anything. In a sense, I felt that I owed Luke so his continuing to pressure me to just let him take me out, led to me going out with him and slipping up after being wined and dined. He was a fine-ass older gentleman and Tristian still wasn't treating me the way that I wanted to be treated, so that led to me sleeping with him a few times when I was being neglected at home. When I got pregnant, I honestly believed my child to be Tristian's, until I pushed her out and saw that she looked just like Luke's ass. It really hurt me that I was probably going to lose Tristian for good this time, so everything that I've done has been for nothing.

"Do you hear me?" I heard his voice reminding me that he was in the room.

"No, what did you say?" I asked him.

"I said, let me hold my daughter," he repeated.

I didn't want him to hold my daughter, but I knew that he wasn't asking and to be honest, I was afraid of what he was going to do if I denied him. I have witnessed some shady conversation while being in his company, so I know what he's capable of if pushed. I handed him my daughter and I'm not going to lie; my heart was beating outside of my chest, scared that he was going to run with my daughter or some shit. I wished that I could call Tristian right now, because I needed him here so that this man didn't do anything stupid. So, while he his attention was on my daughter, I texted Tristian, praying he got the message and came to the hospital.

236

"So, what are you going to name her?" he asked, bringing me out of my thoughts once again.

I had no idea what I was going to name her now that she belonged to someone else, because had she been Tristian's daughter; I was going to name her Ashleigh.

"I have no idea what I'm going to name her," I said with a hint of attitude in my voice, because I just wanted him to leave.

"Well, you need to come up with a name so that I know what to call my daughter," he snapped.

"We don't know that she's your daughter. In case you forgot, I do have a boyfriend that I was fucking pretty much every night," I said, trying to piss him off.

"I already know that he was here and voiced how he wasn't the father of your daughter, so stop with the bullshit. Do you think I would be up here wasting my time if I knew that this was his baby? Look at her; she looks just like her daddy," he smiled at her, kissing her on her forehead.

I sat back, trying to figure out who was telling him my business, and it never dawned on me to ask him how he even knew that I had my baby. Only person that came to mind was Demayo, because she was his brother's ex-girlfriend, but I never told her about Luke and like I said, I just found out that Kylief was her ex.

"How did you know that I had the baby and about Tristian saying that she's not his?" I decided to ask him.

"That's not important, but what is important is you getting the paternity papers together, so that I could sign them. I'll be back up here tomorrow and make sure that you have a name for my pretty girl," he demanded, handing her back to me before leaving out of my room.

Chapter Twenty-Eight
Jess

I finally got Kylief to allow me to call an Uber to go home, under the pretenses that we were still together. It was hard allowing the man responsible for taking two of the most important people in my life to touch me and violate my body, knowing what he done. I was now home, dreading that I had to tell Tristian and Trish that the man I trusted enough to allow in my life; was the man that took their precious mother from them. They both told me to stay away from him and I didn't listen, but I had no idea that he would do something this horrific to me; the person he claimed to love so much. My heart was conflicted because I knew if I told Tristian, he was sure to take Kylief's life and I didn't want his ruining his life on my hands. He's been calling and texting and I knew that it was a matter of time before he came looking for me, so I gave him a call letting him know that I was at my father's house. I had to stop saying my father's house because it was now my house, once I stop playing and move in. I went upstairs to retrieve my bag so that I could give Detective Smalls a call, because I needed to protect Tristian but at the same time, I needed Kylief ass to pay for what he did to Mama Bear and my father.

I swear when I got home, I cried until I couldn't cry anymore, because I blamed myself. *If I had listened and just left him alone; he would have been out of my life.* Nervousness sunk in when I heard the doorbell, because I knew that it was Tristian.

"What's going on? I been trying to get up with you, because you didn't let me know that you made it home. You had a nigga mad worried and stressed at the same time, thinking you linked up with dude," he said in an accusatory tone.

"Well, to be honest with you, when I left the hospital I felt some type of way about her having your firstborn, so I had a few drinks and crashed. When I finally responded to you, I finally got myself together and I'm still feeling it, so I apologize if I had you worried," I lied with a straight face.

I didn't want to lie to him, but I couldn't tell him the truth, and pretending as if I was upset about him having a baby with her was believable.

"Had you answered the phone you would have known that she didn't have my firstborn," he said.

"What do you mean she didn't have your firstborn? Are you trying to say that you have another child?" I asked, confused by what he was saying.

"No, I don't have another child, but that baby that she pushed out isn't my baby, and I put my life on that shit," he said seriously.

"I'm so confused right now," I told him.

"She claimed to be pregnant by me, but the baby that she pushed out looks nothing like me, so I'm assuming she looks like whoever fathered her. The baby is a pretty girl, but she's darker than that shirt you have on and none of her features match mine. I told her that I wanted a DNA test, but I already know what the test is going to say."

"Wow," I responded in disbelief.

"She hit me up, asking me if I could come up to the hospital because dude was up there, and she was scared that he was going to snatch her baby. It's crazy how when I was up there and said to her that the baby wasn't mine and for her to tell me who the father was, he didn't exist," he stressed.

I couldn't tell if he was hurt that she stepped out on him or not, but I could tell that he was disappointed by the tone of his voice.

"I'm so sorry, Tristian," I said, hugging him.

"I'm cool," he lied.

"I know that you're not cool with it, so tell me what I could do to make you feel better," I said, kissing his lips before sticking my tongue in his mouth.

He gripped my ass as we stood in the middle of the living room making out, before he grabbed my hand pulling me behind him. I could feel the butterflies in my stomach dancing around as if this was our first intimate encounter, but I knew it had to do with me being excited to feel him inside of me again. My dad's room was now transformed and fit for the queen that I was, so I couldn't wait to break in my big ass cherry wood, king canopy bed.

"Really?" he questioned, seeing that I had a canopy bed.

"You don't like it? Just wait until the sheer curtains come," I said, causing him to shake his head.

"Let's see how sturdy this bed is," he said, pushing me playfully down on the bed.

He lay on top of me, positioning himself in between my legs and sucking on my neck, before whispering in my ear that he loves me.

"So, you not going to say it back?" he asked.

"Tristian, you already know how I feel about you," I said with a smile, fucking with him because I knew he wanted to hear it.

"So, say that shit," he said tickling me, causing me to laugh hysterically as I twisted my body, begging him to stop as I tried to get away from him.

"Ok, ok, I love you." I gave in, attacking his lips with mine as he used his hands to pull my panties down.

My legs trembled as his tongue had my body ready to convulse, and I grabbed his head once I felt him bite down on my clit.

"Ahh," I moaned as my body jerked, releasing all my juices into his mouth.

"Turn that ass over," he demanded, coming up out of his jeans.

I licked my lips as I got on my knees and scooted my ass in the air, thinking he was about to plunge his big dick in me, but he didn't. He pulled me towards the end of the bed, ass still up in the air as he plunged his face in the crack of my ass, assaulting my ass with his tongue. I couldn't control the feeling he was giving me, and my legs felt weak and ready to collapse as I felt another orgasm rock my ass hard.

"Oh my God, you're trying to kill me; I can barely breathe," I panted.

"Well, that ass better invest in an oxygen mask along with the tank, because I'm going to wear that ass out every time. Now, come sit on this dick," he said, pulling me on top of him. "Fuck, Jess, slow down; I'm not ready to cum yet," he grunted.

I put both hands on his chest and bounced up and down on his dick, ignoring him, because I couldn't slow down if I wanted to. I was riding his dick like a skier riding the slippery slopes and didn't plan on letting up, until I fucked every one of his kids up out of him.

"Yes, just like that. Ahh, fuck this pussy," I cried out as he grabbed my hips, delivering rough deep strokes. "Oh, shit, I'm about to cum," I sang out in pleasure.

He was killing the pussy right, now that he was on the verge of cumming, but the shit felt so fucking good. I collapsed on my back, trying to catch my breath, but his ass already passed out and was snoring lightly. *I put that ass to sleep*, I thought as I got up to shower and that's when I noticed that I had a few missed calls. I took my phone with me into the bathroom and the first voicemail was from Detective Smalls, telling me that Kylief was in custody, but I didn't expect her to just make an arrest. I needed the shit on the news, otherwise, I still would have to break the news to Tristian and Trish and that was something that I didn't want to do. I was praying that the shit hit the news first, since my father and Mama Bear was a big part of the community, with all the charitable programs that they were a part of. After getting out of the shower, I went to cuddle up next to Tristian, hoping that my keeping what I knew from him didn't backfire in my face as I dozed off in his arms.

Chapter Twenty-Nine
Jess

"Jess, wake up," I heard Tristian say, before shaking me out of my sleep.

I rubbed at my eyes, trying to get the sleep out of them, so that I could focus on why Tristian woke me up out of my sleep. After opening my eyes back up and seeing clearly now, I noticed that he was watching the news. My wish came true because right there on my 60-inch television was Kylief's face on the screen, so I sat up so that I could hear what they were saying. I made sure to act just as shocked as Tristian when we heard what the new anchor had to say.

"Turn it up," I said to him because I could barely hear what was being said.

"A man has been arrested in the connection with the murder of a couple that was found dead in their home a few weeks ago. The authorities are reporting that an anonymous tip led them to the home of Kylief James where evidence was found, which in return led to him being taken into custody. You

may remember Kylief James from a few years ago, when his brother, Attorney Luke Bronson, defended him in another murder case of his ex-girlfriend, Alissa Moore, but was cleared of all charges. It's not clear what his motives are for killing retired nurse Trisha Kirkland and her boyfriend, Troy Johnson, but we will keep you updated as we get more information on the case, as this is an ongoing investigation."

So much for acting shocked, because I was in complete shock; so much so that I didn't realize that Tristian was tearing shit up until I heard glass breaking.

"I should have killed that faggot-ass nigga when I had the chance," he yelled as he knocked the lamp off the nightstand. I've seen him angry before, but not this angry and he was scaring me, because he was destroying my bedroom as the tears fell from his eyes. He was now assaulting the wall, so I got up from the spot I was frozen in to try and console him.

"Don't fucking touch me, Jess, this is your fault because you should have left that nigga alone when we were telling you to. My mother and your father's blood is on your hands for being a stupid bitch staying with his ass," he ranted, causing me to get in my feelings.

"Why would you say something so hurtful like that to me, blaming me for something I had no control over" I cried because his words stung.

I had no idea that what Kenya or anyone else said about him was true, and all I did was try not to judge him. I was shocked right now because I had no idea that he was my boss' brother, because he never mentioned it to me. All he told me was that he had two brothers on his father's side but that was it, so I was learning a few more new things that I didn't know about him. Even so, I don't think that Tristian should be saying that their blood was on my hands. I blamed myself, but I never expected him to feel that way, knowing that I had no idea. I'd foolishly believed that Kylief wasn't capable of murdering anyone.

"So, this isn't your fucking fault, Jess? You weren't still fucking with that nigga after that bitch told you what the fuck he did? Huh? Answer the fucking question," he barked, causing me to jump.

His cellphone rung and I knew that it was Trish on the other line, because he was going in on me and trying to calm her down at the same time. I felt like shit because he was right and I just needed to accept that it was my fault. The answer was yes to everything that he'd asked me, but hearing him say it to me and now to Trish crushed me. I needed for them to both know that I would never put them or our parents in danger knowingly, and that it was a bad judgment call on my part.

"Don't tell me what to fucking say, Trish; my fucking mother is dead because of this bitch, acting thirsty for a fucking man," he vented, throwing his phone against the wall.

I walked out of the room going to the other bedroom, because I wasn't going to continue to stand there and take his verbal abuse towards me. I sat in that room for what seemed like forever, until I heard the front door open and close as I let the tears fall from my eyes. Trish had been calling my phone but I wasn't answering, so she sent a text message that I decided to read.

Trish- Jess, pick up the phone so that I could talk to you, because I want you to hear it from my mouth that I don't blame you. Tristian doesn't really blame you, he's just upset and needs someone to blame but trust me, I'm going to make him understand that the only person to blame is Kylief. Call me when you feel like talking and just know that I love you and that will never change.

After reading her message, the tears fell harder as I sat on the bed crying like a baby, knowing that she loved me enough not to blame me. My life as I've known it was over, because learning that Kylief is my boss' brother, so no way was I going back to work there. I finally opened up about my feelings to the only man that I truly loved and now, he's blaming me for us losing our parents. I wanted to believe Trish's words about him just needing someone to blame, but his eyes were so full of hate when he said those words.

I crawled into bed and had been there for the past few hours, not wanting to do anything but I sulked long enough, so I decided to get out of bed. I showered and dressed, before cleaning up the mess that Tristian left in my room, I changed the linen on my bed and picked up the lamp that I was thankful didn't crack. He put a hole in my wall but it wasn't a big hole; nonetheless it was a hole that I was pissed about. I saw his phone in the corner of the room and I expected it to have shattered, but it didn't, probably was because of the thick ass case. Once I was done cleaning my room, I went downstairs to the kitchen to get something to drink, because I was thirsty. Just as I was coming out of the kitchen, someone was knocking at my front door and I started to just let them knock but I thought; *what if it's Tristian*? When I opened the door, it was Detective Smalls with another male detective.

"Hello, Ms. Johnson, can we come in?" she asked.

I allowed them inside, telling them that they could have a seat, before taking a seat myself across from them.

"We just have a few questions that we need to ask," she said.

"Ok."

"As you know, Mr. James is in custody, but we're here to ask if you would be up to coming down to the station to make a statement," she said.

"A statement? Why would I need to make a statement, when you have the evidence that proves he committed the crime?"

"That's just it; we don't think that the evidence will hold up in court and his lawyer could argue that Mr. James has traffic in and out of his home. They will argue that anyone could have put your father's belongings in his home, including you."

"I don't believe this shit. So, does that mean if I don't make a statement that he could walk?" I asked, fear setting in.

"I just want to be totally honest with you, Ms. Johnson; the statement still may not be enough to hold him. The only thing that is bulletproof would be if we had the murder weapon with his prints on them," she said and my heart sunk into my chest.

"If Kylief walks, he's going to know that it was me who sent you to his home and being that he hasn't tried to contact me, he already knows it's me," I cried as panic started to seep in.

"I'm sorry and if it makes you feel any better, we could have a patrol car sit outside of your home, Ms. Johnson," she offered, getting up and rubbing my back.

I now regretted calling her and not letting Tristian handle it, because she was going to get me killed. *If that happened, his ass probably would get off for my murder too, because his brother; my boss is just that damn good*, I thought as my tears continued to fall. I didn't have a choice but to let her know that if my statement wasn't going to keep him in jail, that I wasn't going to come down to the station. She went on to tell me that Kylief would be making bail and if I wanted the patrol car that she suggested earlier, for me to let her know. I really didn't want a patrol car sitting outside of my home, but what other choice did I have? Tristian wasn't speaking to me, so who was going to protect me? So, I told her that I would like for her to have the patrol come and watch my house. I didn't even bother to thank her because I would have been thanking her for absolutely nothing, because she didn't do a damn thing to help me put the bastard away for killing my father and Mama Bear. After I let them out, I picked up my phone to let Trish know what was going on, because I was scared right now. She was the only one I had left to call, so I just hoped she was still feeling the same way she was feeling earlier, about still being here for me.

Chapter Thirty
Kylief

"Why the fuck you can't keep your ass out of trouble, Kylief? How the fuck you go from keeping Jess occupied, to killing her father and soon to be fucking stepmother?" Luke barked, getting on my fucking nerves.

"How many times do I have to tell you that I didn't mean to fucking kill her pops and that I was there to handle her nigga's moms? If that motherfucker didn't put his fucking hands on me, my hand wouldn't have been forced and his mother and her pops would still be breathing," I barked back at his ass.

"Look, you're out on bail so that means stay the fuck out of trouble, because they don't have enough evidence to convict you right now. So, stay away from Jess because if you go and do something stupid while you're out on bail, my nigga, you're on your own," he threatened.

"I hear you," I told him, walking away from him and getting into the car with Demayo.

"So, you're a murderer now?" she laughed, thinking this shit was funny.

"Bitch, don't play with me, just drive this fucking car and don't say shit to me," I barked at her ass.

"That's what your ass gets for fucking with that bitch, with your stupid ass. I knew she was going to be your downfall," she said, not taking heed that she needed to shut up.

"Say one more word and see if I don't knock the shit out of your ass," I warned but knowing her, she wasn't going to leave well enough alone.

She went to say something and I reached over and slapped the shit out of her, causing the car to swerve.

"Nigga, you done lost your fucking mind," she yelled trying to fight me and not paying attention to the road, almost killing us both.

"Pull this motherfucker over now, Demayo," I told her, after getting control of the wheel.

As soon as she pulled the car over; I jumped out, pulling her ass through the passenger side door and tossing her ass on someone's front lawn. I wasn't trying to go back to jail, so I left her ass on the ground cursing and still talking shit. I hopped in her shit and peeled the fuck out, not giving a fuck how she got home, because that's how pissed I was. I always tell her about running her mouth about shit she knows nothing about, yet she just decided to do that shit at the wrong time.

I took my ass straight to the crib and hopped in the shower, because I been in these clothes for over twenty-four hours. I know Luke told me to stay away from Jess, but as soon as I got me a replacement phone, I was going to go by her pop's crib. I wasn't mad at her for snitching on me because had I found out someone took my pop's life, I would have taken theirs or called the authorities, so I understood her position. I just wanted her to know that I didn't know that he was her pops because if I had; I would have never did that shit to her. I didn't want to incriminate myself, but I needed her to know the truth and pray that she forgives me, because I knew that I wasn't going to see any jail time and I still wanted to be with her. I knew that I needed to watch my back, because once that fuck nigga knows that I'm out, he's probably going to be looking for me so I'd make sure that I was strapped.

I made it all the way to Jess' pop's crib, just to see a patrol car chilling out front of the house and I was pissed that I had to wait to see her. I drove past the house, headed towards the next block, got out of the car and going through the backyard of a house that was directly behind her house. I knew that she wasn't going to invite me in, being that she felt she needed protection from me, so I had to jimmy the lock to get inside the house. Her father should have changed the locks on the back door, because that shit was too easy getting in, so she really needed to get that taken care of. I walked up the stairs, making sure that I didn't make noise, because I didn't want to startle her and she starts screaming and then the fuck boys run up in here, when all I'm trying to do is talk to her. I saw the light on in one of the bedrooms, so that's the room that I went to and she was sitting on the bed in the dark watching television. I pushed the door open and walked through and when she saw me, her eyes got big with a fearful look on her face.

"Jess, don't scream; I'm just here to talk to you," I said calmly, letting her know that I wasn't there to cause her harm.

"Kylief, there is a patrol car out front so you need to leave," she said, her voice trembling.

"I know, baby, but you don't need them because I'm not here to hurt you. I just want to talk to you," I told her, trying to get her to calm down.

"I don't have nothing to say to you, Kylief, and I don't understand why you would think that I would talk to you, knowing you killed my father," she cried out.

"Jess, baby; I didn't know that he was your father, because if I knew, I swear I wouldn't have killed him. You never told me that your father was dating your best friend's mother," I pleaded with her.

"You must be crazy if you think that it matters that if you knew you wouldn't have killed him, because you still took the woman who I loved just like a mother," she snapped as the tears now fell from her eyes.

"Look, I'm here to apologize so that we could just move on with our lives, Jess," I said, moving towards her but she put her hand up to stop me.

"Kylief, don't come near me because if you do, I'm going to scream," she warned.

"I told you that I'm not here to hurt you, so you don't have to be scared, Jess, because I just want to be here for you. Why can't you just let me fucking be here for you? Why can't you just be happy that I'm home," I barked, getting pissed because she wasn't trying to hear me.

I was trying not to lose my cool, but she was pushing me to my breaking point, acting like I wasn't standing here apologizing and risking my freedom at the same time. I just want her to hear me out and understand that my hand was forced when it came to pulling that trigger on the nigga's mother. That nigga violated me, so it was only fair to do his ass just as dirty as he did me, when he was in the wrong. He had no business getting in between what I had going on with her, because at the end of the day; she was my bitch, not his. I saw her reach for her phone, so I had no choice but to knock it out of her hand, tackling her on the bed and holding her, because I see that this was the only way to get her to listen.

"Jess, stop fighting and just hear me out please," I begged, but she just kept tussling so I had no choice again when I slapped her.

I wasn't trying to hurt her; I was just trying to calm her down because the situation was getting out of hand. One of her hands got loose and she started scratching at my face and as I went to grab that hand, I let go of the hand that I was holding and she punched me in my eye, causing me to see red as both of my hands were now squeezing the life out of her.

"See what the fuck you made me do," I snapped, squeezing harder until I felt myself being punched in the back of the head.

I fell to the ground and I was now being punched and kicked all over my body, so all I could do at this point was cover my face.

"Get the fuck up, nigga, and fight like a fucking man," I heard Tristian's voice as he kicked me in my face.

The anger in me was on one thousand as I attempted to stand and fell back down, but not before reaching for my gun.

"So, you're not as tough as you thought, bitch-ass nigga, get the fuck up and fight a real nigga," he said, coming towards me and I pulled the trigger.

"Tristian, nooooooo," Jess cried out.

The first shot didn't drop him, so when I saw him reaching for what I believed was a gun, I pulled the trigger again. He grabbed his chest, falling to the floor, and everything from there was in slow motion as I saw Jess crying over his body, with officers now telling me to drop my weapon. I couldn't believe that all this shit happened when all I was trying to do was apologize to her ass, but now I regret the day I met her. She made me love her and that wasn't part of the plan when I agreed to do this solid for my brother, *but everything good comes to an end*, I thought as I put the gun to my head and pulled the trigger.

Chapter Thirty-One
Demayo

"Damn, that bitch done knocked you off your square, just like I tried to warn you but you just wouldn't listen. So, you try to kill yourself and couldn't even get that shit right. Fucking pathetic," I spat at Kylief's comatose ass as he lay handcuffed to the hospital bed.

Don't ask me why they have his ass handcuffed when he's in a coma and has been for a few weeks now. I was with Luke the night he got the call about Kylief. After he dragged me out of my car, I had to knock on the door of the house he left me at to use the phone. Not only did he take my car, he drove off with my purse and my cell phone, so it was crazy how I had sympathy for him when I heard what happened. I was pissed off with him now that he would do this to himself behind a bitch that didn't give a shit about him.

"Why the fuck would you do this, Kylief?" I demanded as I punched him in his chest, letting my tears fall. "This shit is just so unfair that you would be so selfish and try to take your life, what about me? Didn't I love you? I pleaded with you to just let that girl be, but no; you went and fell in love with the bitch. I just don't understand why you were even looking for love, when love was right in your face the whole fucking time. I hate you, Kylief, I fucking hate you." I bawled over him like he could hear and answer me.

I just couldn't wrap my brain around why he just couldn't be content with me, when I've done so much to prove my love for him. A lot of people don't know that I'd been in Kylief life as his friend before being in a relationship with him. Twin didn't even know of the history that I had with him, because that's the way Kylief wanted it. When his ex-girlfriend, Serena, put an order of protection out on him, I handled it. When that bitch, Kenya, who he was still fucking, went running her mouth to Jess, I handled it. When he pillow-talked about how his brother, Luke, didn't give him his part of the insurance money that was supposed to be split between all three of them but it didn't happen, I was in the process of handling that too. I've done so much for this man and he had no idea; all that I've done for him and all that I would have continued to do for him. Now he was lying in this bed helpless and there's nothing I could do to help him and that shit hurts me to my core. I hate looking at him because this was just a shell of him; Kylief

James was no longer here, so it made no sense keeping him on this machine that was breathing for him. I knew that I had to do what I needed to do, so that the love of my life could be at peace, so I kissed him on his lips and walked out of the room just as the hospital staff was rushing in. Seeing the officer at the door standing there like Kylief was going to get up and try to escape pissed me off.

"Where the fuck you rushing to like you pigs don't know he's in a fucking coma? How about you run your ass up in there and remove those cuffs, bitch?" I shouted before waking to the elevator.

When I got outside the hospital, my tears fell at the finality that he was gone and I was never going to see him again. When I got inside my car my phone started ringing, so I dug down in my bag and once I retrieved it, I saw that it was Luke calling. I let the call go straight to voicemail because now that my love was gone there was no need to continue like I cared for his ass. I felt bad for Kylief's mother because she had no one now and even if I tried to be there for her, I already know that she wasn't going to allow me to because she doesn't care for me. It was all good though, because I have no plans on staying in New York. There's too many bad memories here, so I needed to end this chapter and start another one. I pulled up to my building and stepped out of the car and by the time I heard the tires screeching, it was too late as the car hit me, sending my body in the air before hitting the ground.

Chapter Thirty-Two
Jess

I woke up yawning and stretching from the same spot I've been sleeping in since Tristian had been shot. You would think that the hospital would offer a cot or something for me to sleep on, being that they allowed me to be here with him all this time. The only time I leave the hospital is when Trish comes to sit with him, so that I could go home to shower and change my clothes. He was shot twice in the chest with both bullets being removed, but he slipped into a coma and hasn't awakened yet. The doctors expect a full recovery as his body has already begun to recover, but as far as him waking up, they said he must do that on his own. I have been on an emotional roller coaster since it all happened, because once again; I've been silently blaming myself. When I got the call from Kylief's mother that he expired, my heart went out to her and I even cried a few tears for him too. I made a promise to myself that I was going to keep in touch with her, because she had no one now. I know that I didn't owe him that to look after her, but it was something my heart wouldn't allow me not to do for her.

Trish called to say that she wasn't going to make it up to the hospital for another twenty minutes, telling me to go home. She said that she was sure that he would be ok until she got there, because she knew that I never wanted to leave him alone, just in case he woke up. When he did decide to wake up, I wanted him to wake up to a familiar face, just in case he woke up disoriented. Just as I did every morning before leaving him, I walked over to his bed, kissing him on the lips and telling him that I was leaving, but I'd return.

My house didn't feel like a home because I'm hardly here, and I haven't been cleaning or anything, but I would have to worry about that once Tristian wakes up. That seemed to be my only focus these days and most days I don't even eat, because that's how worried I am about him. I wasn't feeling well and would have loved to take a nap in my bed, but that wasn't going to happen because I needed to get back to the hospital. I did make me ham and cheese omelet with some orange juice, before heading back to the hospital to be with my love.

When I walked into his room, I didn't see Trish but Toni was sitting in the chair beside his bed, with his hand in hers. I had no idea why she was here but what I did know was she needed to make her exit, because Tristian no longer belonged to her. I have no idea where I stood with him right now, but that didn't mean I was going to allow her to be here holding his hand, like they were good before this happened. Trish was supposed to be here and this was another reason I didn't like to leave him alone, because of all the trolls that have been trying to visit him. A few I knew from high school and a few I didn't know, but they were coming up here like it was his damn wake or something, so I shut them all down. Now here I was, being put in the position to shut another one down and don't get me wrong; he cared for her and I'm sure she cared for him too, so her seeing him wasn't the problem. Her being up in here like they were still in a relationship was the problem I was having.

"Toni, why are you here?" I asked her.

"The same reason you're here," she said, saying no more.

"What I mean is, why are you here when he wasn't rocking with you before being shot?" I rephrased it for her.

"Look, it doesn't matter if he was rocking with me or not. I have been up here every day to see him," she said.

"I've never seen you here and I've been here with him since the day the shit happened, so how the fuck was you here?" I snapped.

"Don't you go home every morning? Yes, you do, so when I know that you're not here, I come to see him to avoid exactly what's happening now," she said and I got pissed because if she was coming up here, Trish was allowing her to.

"I'm confused as to why you feel you're entitled to be here to see him, when you just tried to pin a fucking baby on him," I said, getting angrier by the second.

"What does that have to do with the way I feel about him? I could go on and say some shit about you but I won't, because that wouldn't change how you feel about him. My being here shouldn't be a problem and I shouldn't have to sneak in to see him like I'm doing something wrong. And for the record, I didn't pin a baby on him because in my heart, I believed it to be his baby," she responded, letting go of his hand to wipe a few tears that fell.

Just as I was about to respond to her, my boss, Luke, walked into the room and now I was wondering what the fuck he was doing here. I haven't seen or spoken to him since the day that I went into the office to quit and take my belongings. I just knew that he was going to say something to me, so when he walked over to Toni, I was even more confused when he grabbed her by her arm. I don't know why he thought it would be ok to bring this drama to the hospital where Tristian is recovering, but they both needed to leave.

"So, this is the reason you needed me to stay home this morning with my daughter?" he said to her.

"Your daughter?" I asked in shock as to what the fuck was going on.

"Luke, I'm not in a relationship with you, so my reason for leaving your daughter with you has nothing to do with you," she snapped at him.

"Does anybody want to tell me what the hell is going on?" I wanted to know.

"I doubt if she wants you to know how the two of us met," he smirked and now I was curious to what he wasn't saying.

"Luke, you need to leave and where the hell is my daughter anyway?" she said to him.

"I'm more interested in why he said that you wouldn't want me to know how you two met, so do you want to tell me what that has to do with me?' I asked her.

"Luke is the reason for you and Kylief being together," she said, but she needed to come better than that.

"How you figure?" I asked her.

"I bumped into Luke not paying attention, thinking he was a nice man because he seemed sincere when he asked me if I wanted to talk about what was bothering me. After telling him about what was going on in my relationship with Tristian, that's when he offered to help me with a distraction. By distraction, he meant find someone who would occupy your time, so that you wouldn't spend all of your free time with Tristian. At the time, I was desperate, so I agreed and when I told him who you were, that's when I learned that you worked for him. Like I said, I was desperate so I didn't let that deter me from going through with it, so your meeting Kylief at his law firm that morning wasn't a chance meeting. We never expected Kylief to fall for you; all I wanted was some me time with Tristian, without him blowing me off to spend time with you," she finished.

"Wow, so how did that work out for you?" I asked, being sarcastic.

I wanted to be upset but to be honest; at this point I didn't even care anymore about anything but Tristian opening his eyes. I didn't care what she had going on with Luke, because it wasn't my business and that's something that she needed to handle. I stood for a few minutes watching them go back and forth with each other, wishing that they would both just leave. He went on to tell her that she needed him, because Tristian didn't want her and that Demayo was fucking him and that's how he knew her every move. I'd never seen her with an aggressive bone in her body, but she lost it and attacked his ass. I couldn't believe that this grown ass man was on this childish bullshit and I was thankful when they were being escorted out of the hospital. I swear, when you think you know a person, you have no fucking idea who they really are until it's too late. I was just so over everyone and from this day forward, I'm going to be careful about whom I trust and that means everyone. I walked over to the bed, apologizing to Tristian for the altercation that just happened in his room, because I heard coma patients can hear what goes on around them. I was now sitting near the window going through my phone. When Trish walked in the room and she saw the pissed look on my face, she tried to avoid eye contact.

"So, when were you going to tell me that you were allowing Toni to visit with Tristian?" I asked her.

"I didn't say anything because I knew that you were going to have a problem with it," she said.

"You damn right, why wouldn't I have a problem with it? He wasn't with her when the shit happened."

"It doesn't matter if he was with her or not, Jess, because she still cared for him, so how would it look for me to tell her that she couldn't see him?"

"Trish, I don't have a problem with her seeing him, but her up here holding his hand and expressing her love for him, yes; I have a problem with that," I snapped.

"Well, I didn't know that she was doing all of that, but like I said, who was I to deny her from seeing him?"

"Well, you won't have to worry about denying her, because I told the bitch not to come back again. She just sat here and admitted that my meeting Kylief was a set-up between her and my boss, Luke, who happens to be her baby father, might I mention. Had she not been so fucking jealous of my relationship with your brother, none of this shit would have happened, because I would have never met Kylief." I cried as soon as the words left my mouth.

I was just so tired and so fucking annoyed that Toni would do something like this, instead of just putting her foot down. I never forced Tristian to spend more time with me than he wanted to spend at home; I even kicked his ass to the curb so that he could go home most times. So, I just hope that her ass takes ownership of some of this blame that's been weighing heavily on my mind since this shit happened.

"I'm sorry, Jess, I had no idea," she expressed, trying to console me as I was having a breakdown.

"I'm just so torn up right now, Trish, because we lost so much and now your brother is in a coma and we have no idea when or if he's going to wake up. I know you keep telling me not to blame myself, but it's so hard not to when I see him lying in that bed, knowing Kylief put him there," I stressed to her.

"I don't know how to stop you from feeling that way, but what I will do is remind you of this to give you something to think about. Kylief pulled the trigger that killed our parents, Kylief is the person who attacked you, and Kylief is the person that shot my brother twice."

Chapter Thirty-Three
Trish

I finally got Jess to calm down and we were now using Tristian's meal table to play cards, but Jess still seemed as if her mind was on something else.

"Jess, it's your pull," I said to her.

"My bad," she said, pulling a card and looking at it briefly before throwing it down, not realizing that she threw down a wild card.

"Jess, dammit, are you playing or not?" I laughed at her.

"What?" she asked and I pointed to the wild card. "I'm sorry, girl, my mind is all over the place," she apologized.

"It's ok, we could play another time," I told her, taking the cards from her and placing them in the box.

Now thumbing through my phone, I could have sworn I saw movement from Tristian out the corner of my eye, but chalked it up to me bugging.

"Oh shit," I blurted out, causing Jess to jump.

"What?" she questioned, nervously looking around; I guess trying to see what I was talking about.

"Yo, Jess, I swear I just saw him move." I jumped up, going towards the bed with her following me.

"Oh my God," Jess squealed, covering her mouth as her tears fell.

Tristian's eyes were fluttering as if he was trying to get them to focus and once he opened his eyes, I tried to get him to respond to my voice. He didn't respond and it looked like he was just staring off into space, with me waving my hand in front of his face. After a few seconds of trying to get him to respond, he started pulling at the IV that was in his arm and that's when I told Jess to go and get someone. When she turned to walk out, his eyes followed her so I didn't understand why he wasn't responding to me. When the doctor came into the room, I told him that Tristian's eyes followed Jess as she left out of the room. He tried to explain something about visual and auditory tracking, which is a sign of improvement and that if Tristian was doing it already, it meant he was improving rather aggressively. Every command that the doctor gave him he followed, but he still hasn't spoken yet, leaving me to believe that he couldn't or he just didn't want to. After the doctor left out of the room, I tried to get him to speak again but he still wasn't responding. Jess wasn't saying anything, just staring at him and causing him to turn his head. It clicked to me that he wasn't talking because she was in the room, so I pulled her to the side and asked her if she could step out for a second. She looked at me strangely but she did as I asked her, because I told her I would explain in a second. His eyes once again watched her as she exited the room, so I was almost positive that his ass didn't want her here.

"Why is she here?" he asked, just above a whisper but I heard him.

"She's been here every day since you've been here, Tristian," I told him, but he didn't respond. "Tristian, please don't blame her because it's not her fault, and I need you to stop blaming her for this. She blames herself too, but I've been trying to convince her that she's not to blame for Kylief's actions," I offered an explanation, but he still didn't respond and was now staring off into space again.

"So, he doesn't want me here?" Jess asked from the door, standing there with tears in her eyes.

I felt bad for her and I didn't want to tell her that he didn't want her here but I didn't have to once I saw that she turned her head no longer looking at me. She came into the room and grabbed her bag and phone before leaving out of the room, pissed that Tristian was treating her this way. She sat by his side the entire time that he was in this hospital so she didn't deserve to be treated this way. So, now I guess he was upset with me too, because he wasn't speaking or making eye contact with me now, so I gave him that. I went to sit back in the chair giving my phone my attention and his ass the silent treatment, until he decided he wanted to talk to me.

After an hour passed by, the nurse was back in the room attending to him, asking him about his pain level. I wasn't Jess, so I wasn't staying the night at the hospital, especially when his ass wasn't speaking to me. I told him that I was going home and would be back tomorrow to see him when I got off work, but his stubborn ass still didn't say anything so I just left, hoping he has a better attitude tomorrow. When I got outside the hospital, I saw that Jess didn't leave. Instead, she was sitting on the bench, looking torn with tears streaming down her face, causing my tears to fall. I hated seeing her like this because her being hurt, hurts me and I just wish that Tristian would come around.

"Jess, you have to stop doing this to yourself, Look, you haven't gotten any rest since this happened. Come back to the house with me so that you could get some rest," I pleaded with her.

"No, I'm ok. Trish, just go home and thank you," she said.

"Jess, I'm not leaving you out here like this," I told her.

"Trish, I'm ok; I promise, so go home and I'll call you tomorrow," she tried to convince me.

I didn't want to leave her, but she wasn't trying to leave with me, so I told her that I loved her and I would check up on her tomorrow. My brother crushed her and it was written all over her face. I never knew her to want to cause harm to herself, but it did cross my mind. I was going to make sure to call her once I got to the house to make sure that she left and made it home. Maybe she did just need some time to herself, so I decided that I wasn't going to push the issue and just let her be for now. After being home for a few hours, I called Jess' phone but it just kept going to voicemail, causing me let out an exasperated breath.

"Still no answer?" Mekhi asked and I wanted to say so badly, *do you hear me talking to her,* but I didn't.

I didn't want to take my frustration out on him, so I just took a deep breath and just answered his question. "No, she didn't answer her phone, still going to voicemail," I stressed.

"Try not to stress too much, because I'm sure that she's ok. Heartbroken, but ok," he tried to convince me.

"I just hope that's the case, because I really wouldn't be the same if something happens to her. I just wish that she would just answer to say that she's ok," I told him.

Jess was known for shutting people out when she was going through something, because she never wants to be a burden on anyone. That's why I stressed to her that if she needed me, I was just a phone call away, whenever she was going through something this hurtful. I picked my phone back up and left her a detailed message, just letting her know that I love her and to call me as soon as she feels like talking.

Chapter Thirty-Four
Jess

After seeing Rome and Ramel leaving the hospital, I knew that I'd sat on this bench pondering my decision long enough. I wasn't shedding another damn tear over Tristian's ass because clearly, my tears meant nothing to him. Three fucking weeks straight I was there, talking to him, massaging him and even helping the nurses wash him, so for him to fix his face to say he doesn't want me there, I'd already been there. As soon as I got off the elevator, my nerves were trying to get the best of me now that I stood outside of his room door. I bit my bottom lip, taking a deep breath before going inside, but he appeared to be sleeping and as I got closer to the bed, he was indeed asleep. I went to take my spot on the uncomfortable sleeper chair that has become my bed, scrolling on my phone. I saw that Trish sent me a text message so since he was sleeping, I just texted her back to let her know that I was ok and made sure to thank her again. Just as I got comfortable and about to doze off, the nurse came into the room and I was pissed that she woke Tristian up. I wasn't prepared for the conversation that I wanted to have with him, so I prayed that she stuck around until I was able to get my thoughts together. All she did was check his vitals before leaving out of the room and now his eyes were focused on me, making me nervous because like I said, I wasn't ready.

"How are you feeling?" I asked him, but he didn't respond.

"How long are you going to be mad with me, Tristian? I was here every day because I was scared that I was going to lose you," I confessed to him, but he still didn't say anything.

I felt like just getting up and walking out, but I wasn't leaving because that's what he wanted, so if he wanted to play the mute game I was going to play it with him. I picked my phone back up, scrolling through Facebook and trying my best not to let him see how I was really feeling. Out the corner of my eye, I kept seeing him sneak glances, but I wasn't going to say anything else to his ass. He would have to say something to me because I wasn't about to initiate another conversation, just for him not to say shit to me.

"Why are you here, Jess, knowing that I don't want you here?" he finally spoke.

"Tristian, why don't you want me here?" I asked him.

"You already know why I don't want you here, Jess," he said.

"So, you still blaming me for what happened to our parents, even though you know that I had no control over what happened?"

"If you would have just left that nigga alone, we wouldn't even be having this conversation."

"Do you think it was that easy to just leave him alone when I was already feeling him? Why do I have to be at fault because I gave him the benefit of the doubt, believing everything that he was telling me? Isn't that what you do when you care for a person?" I asked him, because he's acting like he never made a damn mistake before in trusting someone who shouldn't have been trusted.

If he wanted to get technical, I can call his ass out on trusting that Toni was faithful to him all this damn time, and believing that she was pregnant with his baby.

"Tristian, it wasn't a day that went by that I didn't blame myself for what happened, until Trish helped me understand that I'm not to blame. Kylief was the one who killed our parents, Kylief was the one that pulled the trigger and shot you, not Jess, so from this day forward I don't care who feels the need to blame me. I loved your mother, my father and I even loved your ass, so do you honestly think that I would put any of you guys' lives in danger knowingly?" I cried, breaking my promise not let another tear fall.

"You said loved as in past tense, does that mean you don't love me anymore?" he asked me and I released a smile through my tears.

"Come here," he said, but I hesitated. "I'm sorry," he apologized.

I got up and walked over to him and he pulled me into his arms, hissing from the pain of me now lying on his chest. I tried to move because he was clearly in pain, but he pulled me back into him.

"I'm sorry," he said again in my ear and I let my tears fall.

He really hurt me but I allowed him to kiss my tears away, letting him know that I accepted his apology. He was breathing like he was short of breath and I knew that it had to do with me lying on his chest. I moved from lying on his chest and he took a few deep breaths like it was a relief, causing me to laugh.

"So, you were just gone let me kill you? You're breathing hard like you about to take your last breath."

"Nah, I'm good, it hurts to breathe whether you were on my chest or not," he said.

"Do you want me to get the nurse so that she could give you something for the pain?" I asked, concerned that he was in pain.

"Nah, but you could answer my question."

"And what question might that be, Tristian?" I asked, already knowing.

"Do you still love me?"

"Tristian, if I didn't love you, I wouldn't be here knowing you didn't want me here," I told him.

"I already know; I just wanted you to say it. When I got shot, I heard you sounding like O-Dog from *Menace II Society* when he was like, 'stay up, Caine, don't die, Caine,'" he laughed.

"That's not funny, Tristian; I thought you were going to die, so you damn right I was telling you not to die on me. Why were you at the house anyway after you went all the way off on me?"

"I knew that you needed me, don't ask me how I knew but I knew," he said, taking my hand in his. "I'm sorry, Jess, and I really do hope that you forgive me for all the hurtful things that I said to you. I was angry and needed someone to blame and being that you were there, I blamed you. So, do you forgive me?"

"I guess, since I forgave you for treating me like you didn't want me here, I could forgive you for blaming me too. I just need for us to lean on each other, because we are all going through the same pain of losing our loved ones," I told him, getting emotional again.

"I love you, Jessica Johnson."

"I love you too, Tristian Kirkland," I said, reaching over and kissing him on his lips.

Tristian was released from the hospital about a week later, so I was thankful for that because he was even looking better. My first night home in my bed, I slept for like two days straight that how much my body missed my bed. Tristian was over here today, fixing the hole he put in my wall as he promised, so I was downstairs making him some lunch. I was frying him some chicken dipped in pancake mix, since he stressed how much he missed me making it for him. I took the waffle iron out, because we were having Jess' chicken and waffles up in this bitch today. Trish said that she and Mekhi were on their way, so I made sure to make enough for them too. Tristian was finished plastering so he said that he was going to take a shower so that meant that I was going to have to set the table. As I was putting the syrup and ketchup on the table, Trish walked her ass in my door, like I didn't tell her ass about inviting herself in my home.

"Are you serious, Trish? I told you about using your key when I home, because you're going to fuck around and get shot. You know my nerves are bad after everything that went down," I told her ass.

"Girl, you ain't shooting shit with your scary ass and you should know by now that if I got a key, I'm using it," she responded, walking her ass in the kitchen, inviting herself to a piece of chicken.

"So, you couldn't wait until you washed your hands, to be all up in my kitchen and my food?" I rolled my eyes, pushing her ass out. "Excuse my manners, Mekhi, but your girl in here acting like she doesn't have any home training." I laughed.

"It's all good," he smiled, shaking his head at Trish, who was now dipping her chicken into the syrup.

We all ate and was now enjoying each other company as we played a game of spades with Trish and Mekhi talking shit because we were beating them by two games now. I loved to play spades but haven't played in a long time but I see it was just like riding a bike once you learn you never forget. I could tell that Trish was feeling good off the few glasses of Rose she'd been drinking because she was becoming touchy feely at the table with Mekhi.

They left about an hour later so Tristian and I was just chilling in the living room watching a movie. He kept looking at his watch like he had somewhere to be so me letting my insecurities get the best of me I was just going to ask him.

"Do you have somewhere to be?" I asked turning to look at him.

"Nah, I was just seeing how much longer we had until the movie was over." he said causing me to shoot daggers his way.

"If you didn't like the movie you could have said something." I told him.

"I love the movie but I want to play something for you so if you don't mind could you put the movie on pause for a second."

I put the movie on pause and that's when he stood picking up his phone going through his phone then pausing to say something.

"Look, I'm not good with words so if you will allow me to play this song for you and don't hold this against me because I'm about to get my corny on.

"I promise that I will not hold it against you only if I like the song and what you're trying to say to me." I smiled waiting for him to play the song.

"I found love in you, and I've learned to love me too.

Never have I felt that I could be all that you see.

It's like our hearts have intertwined and to the perfect harmony.

This is why I love you, oh, this is why I love you.

Because you love me, you love me.

I found love in you.

And no other love will do.

That's why I love you.

I rocked back and forth as the tears fell from my eyes because this song was beautiful and so were the words. My hand covered my mouth and my eyes squinted to make sure that I was seeing clearly as I watched him kneel in front of me with a ring box in his hand. He allowed the song to continue to play but turned it down and I swear to you I was doing one of those ugly cries with my shoulders heaving up and down because I swear this was so unexpected. Even when he asked to play a song for me I had no idea he planned to do this and thinking about mama bear, pops or even Trish not being here for this moment made those tears fall even harder. I knew I needed to give him my attention before his ass stood and I lost out on what she was about to say.

"Jess, you already know that I'm a man of a few words so I'm not going to drag this out so will you accept this ring and be my wife." he said and once I said yes Trish crazy ass came from the kitchen screaming and jumping up and down like a damn fool.

She was hugging me and holding on to me tight expressing how happy she was but I needed her to move so I could get to my man. I didn't even notice the camera that was set up on top of my wall until Tristian told Mekhi that he could stop it. I'm all for memories but I didn't want nobody seeing me crying like that on the video because like I said it was an ugly cry.

"So, you just full of surprises huh?" I asked him as he now held me in his arms.

"I have another surprise for that ass as soon as Trish and her dude leave." he said loud enough for them to hear.

"Oh, so my services are no longer needed I see." she said to him as she feigned like he hurt her feelings.

"You know I love you sis but you know how this shit goes." he winked at her.

"Anyway, congrats again and I'll get up with you freaks later." she said taking Mekhi by the hand telling him we were kicking them out.

He gave Tristian a manly hug congratulating him before leaving out the door with Trish who was still fussing. I locked the door behind her and as soon as I walked back into the living room his ass was all over me. We took our flirting to the bedroom where he made slow passionate love to me making sure to be gentle as he once again expressed his love for me. My heart pounding in my chest as he pounded in and out of me whispering in my ear that he wanted me to have his baby. He didn't even know that the night that we shared at my father house that he already planted his seed but with all that's been going on I didn't have the chance to tell him or wanted to tell him after he blamed me for everything.

"I'm already having your baby." I said and she stopped mid stroke to look at me.

"I'm sure and it's yours." I told him because I didn't want him to have any doubts that this baby belonged to Kylief.

"I love you." he hissed as he kissed me deeply as he continued to give me long gentle strokes until we both came with him collapsing on his back and me laying on his chest thinking of all the future held for us.

I swear that anytime I expressed my feelings letting a man know how I felt about them it always ending with my feelings getting hurt and this time was no different. Tristian was one of those men that hurt me to my core but the only difference is that he made the decision to right his wrong. I knew that I made the right decision to forgive him because as soon as the words left my lips I felt the stress of the world leave my body.

I've made mistakes in my life and had I lived by that statement that my teacher from my Life Skills class tried to instill in me I might have avoided some of the pain I endured. She said that sometimes you have to do what's best for you and your life, not what's best for everybody else. I may have not listened back then but from this day on those are the words I'm going to live by.

The End…